KATINA

THE MERMAID WHO WANTED TO BE HUMAN

(CURSES and SPELLS of THE OLD WATER WITCH)
(As the sea-legend has it written)

Written, Illustrated and Edited
by

Shirley Ruth Hassen

Co-edited
by

Shirley-ann Greenhalgh

Penned © 1956

Copyright ©2019 Shirley Ruth Hassen

Other books by Author
Mixed stories for Girls
Mixed stories for Boys
Justice Prevails
One Only
Hearts' Bondage revealed
Elocin and Zab
EBook – GEORGE AND THE AUTHOR

EMAIL: Shirley.hassen@gmail.com

Contents

Dedication vii
Synopsis viii

Chapter One (Tom and Katie) 1
Chapter Two (Deep below the sea) 7
Chapter Three (King Enahs and Lorac's Wedding) 11
Chapter Four (Dearra's heart's desire) 15
Chapter Five (Tan swims to the top of the ocean) 20
Chapter Six (Queen Coral felt something pulling on her tail) 24
Chapter Seven (The sea world accepts Katina) 29
Chapter Eight (Katina asked, "Mother? Why am I not like other
　　　　　　　　 mermaids?") 34
Chapter Nine ("Why is my mermaid looking so sad") 38
Chapter Ten (Remembering it was Marla's birthday) 43
Chapter Eleven 51
Chapter Twelve (Marla will think me truly brave when I tell her I
　　　　　　　　 swam close to a boat) 54
Chapter Thirteen 57
Chapter Fourteen (Mother … I know where Katina has gone!) 63
Chapter Fifteen ("Katina! We must send you back to the ocean
　　　　　　　　 because …") 67

Chapter Sixteen (Marla? Does the old water witch and the old crone still live?) 76

Chapter Seventeen ("No! Not my beautiful hair!") 85

Chapter Eighten (Marla, I must say goodbye to you now.") 95

Chapter Nineteen (I heard our little mermaid singing) 104

Chapter Twenty (The strange feeling in her feet as she stood caused Katina to giggle) 109

Chapter Twenty One (Breaking the old water witch's curses) 115

Dedication

I DEDICATE KATINA TO my wonderful family for their believing I would one day have my KATINA story published. I give a special "Thank You" to my daughter Shirley-ann and Peter, my friends and relations who had confidence in my books. A special thank you to son-in-law Peter Toneman. Thanks to grand-children, Kathie and Michael for coming to my rescue when my internet collapsed.

Synopsis

KATINA
(The mermaid who wanted to be a human)

TOM, A FISHERMAN, lives with his wife Katie in a small thatch-roofed house. Not young they dearly wished to have a child to love. Tom is often sick but still goes out in his boat to net his fish. Tom's catches are not many, catching enough fish for him and Katie, with a few left to sell at the markets. It is in the ocean that a mer-baby is rescued by the mermaid Queen, Coral. Queen Coral seeing the mer-baby's black-hair is startled but soon forgets her shock when seeing the baby is of the sea. With her King she claims the mer-baby as their own. King Trebor names the mer-child, Katina. Katina grows into a mischievous mer-maid. Katina disobeys her mother's warnings about going to the top of the ocean and is caught in a fisherman's net. Katina lives many years with Tom and Katie when Katie notices Katina's sadness. Although it breaks Tom and Katie's hearts, they send Katina back to her people. Katina grows into a beautiful Siren. Katina is happy with her people but misses Tom and Katie. Going to the old crone for advice, Katina is shocked by the old crone's words. "Cut off your hair and give it to me!" "Please! No! Old crone! Not my beautiful hair?" Give me your hair or no human body for you!" Cutting off her hair, Katina places it in the pearly shell the old crone pushes to her. As the old crone turns to leave, Katina wails, "How will I reach the shore?" Waving a gnarled finger the old crone causes a high wave to speed Katina to the shore. Katina waits near the sea shore for her body to become human. Believing the old crone has lied to her Katina hides herself by day. For two nights Katina wails until she finally sleeps.

Chapter One
(Tom and Katie)

ONCE UPON A TIME … in a quiet, peaceful fishing village in Austria, there lived a poor fisherman named Tom. Now Tom lived with his good wife Katie, in a small old brick thatch-roofed cottage. Their cottage was close to the ocean shore which made it easy for Tom to moor his small fishing boat and return to his home without putting further strain on his health.

Although Tom and Katie had been married many years they did not have any children. As much as they both dearly wanted a child, it was not to be, but they were very happily contented being with each other.

Tom and Katie were not young and Tom was often ill. But as ill as Tom was, he would take his boat out and manage to catch a few fish. Tom's boat was small and old and it was not as grand as the other fishermen's boats, but it served his fishing needs. His boat also not being as strong as the others, Tom did not row as far from the shore as the other fishermen did.

Having no children to take care of and while Tom was away fishing, Katie busied herself keeping their cottage clean.

Katie also busied herself digging in her garden. It was often, while digging in her small garden, that she would admire her neighbour's gardens with the many beautiful colourful flowers.

It was on a day when Tom had been too ill to take his boat out that Katie had set a chair beside the long wide, thin curtained window for him to look out at the warm day. From the window Tom watched Katie working happily in her small garden. Knowing Katie's desire to have gardens along her fences like her neighbours, it was that afternoon when he was feeling better that he dug several long narrow gardens along their fences.

When Katie saw her gardens ready for planting flowers, her pleasure was so great that she kissed Tom on his cheek. Hoping Tom had not made himself sicker, Katie said, "Thank you Tom. Now my gardens will look just like the neighbours' gardens."

…But! Alas! No matter how much care Katie took in her garden, her flowers did not grow like her neighbours.

AND … so it was … that one day Katie asked her neighbour Tina, "Tina! Why do your flowers grow so beautiful when mine do not?"

Pointing to the sad looking soil, Tina told Katie, "Only certain flower seeds grow in such salty ground." Seeing Katie's sadness, Tina gave a light laugh and then cheerfully said, "You wait here and I will give you a handful of my seeds, for you to grow." Hurrying inside her house, Tina was soon giving Katie a handful of seeds.

A smiling Katie said, "Thank you Tina. I will plant them today."

The seeds safe in her clenched fist, humming happily, Katie hurried to Tom's neatly-dug garden plots and carefully planted the seeds, Watching his Katie, Tom smiled at his now happy wife.

Taking several weeks for the seeds to start growing, soon they grew into healthy plants. Soon flower buds grew. Kati felt so happy as the buds grew into many beautiful flowers and her once bare flower beds were as colourful as her neighbours. The rainbow of colours gave their cottage a magical rainbow look … and so Katie spent her days happily cleaning their cottage and attending her gardens.

Tom spent his days fishing.

Katie and Tom being poor did not worry Katie but sadly, Tom wanting to give Katie more than he did, their being poor worried him.

Loving Tom as she did, Katie worried more for his health than for having riches. Being a Christian and loving God, Katie believed that loving each other rather than money was the most important thing in their lives.

As time passed for the elderly Katie and Tom, Katie enjoyed giving Tom surprises. One time she surprised him with a jumper she had secretly been knitting. The jumper had taken many months to knit but now it was finished Kati gave it to Tom.

Tom's look of pleasure made Katie know the long hours knitting the jumper was worth while.

Secretly Tom had known about the jumper but would not think of spoiling Katie's pleasure when she gave it to him. As Katie gave him the Jumper, he said, "The jumper will keep me warmer while I am fishing." Kissing her on the forehead he spoke soft, "Thank you Katie." Tom did not let Katie know he had seen the many stitches she had dropped and sewed together with the same twine.

Tom, in his turn brought Katie shells from the beach for her collection. Katie lovingly placed the shells along her garden borders. The new shell Tom now gave Katie was no bigger than the other ones but it was truly the most colourful. "Oh! Tom! This shell is the prettiest you have ever given me! It is as though a mermaid had put it on the sand especially for you to find for me!"

Grinning at Katie, Tom teased, "You are always imagining such wonderful thoughts." Tom again teased Katie, "Whatever would you do Katie, if I truly did bring your imaginary mermaid home?"

Giving a short soft laugh, Katie teasingly answered, "A little mermaid would make me very happy thank you, Tom!"

Playing Katie's game, Tom asked, "And what would you do with such a mermaid should I bring her home to you?"

Excitedly Katie said, "Oh! Tom! If it were truly possible to own a mermaid, I would love her dearly as our own."

Hugging Katie to him, Tom whispered, 'And I, my wonderful Katie, would also love her as our own."

Pushing Tom gently from her, Katie kindly roused, "Now then, Tom! You know there are no such sea creatures as mermaids even though we humans do believe in the superstitious saying, "Whoever finds a mermaid, much good luck will be theirs."

It was after many long weary hours of fishing Tom would catch just enough fish to feed him and Katie, with a few small fish left to sell for a cheap price to the market. The money collected from the markets barely put food in Katie's cupboards.

Although Katie and Tom's lives continued to be poor, loving each other dearly, Katie and Tom's lives were very happy.

Chapter Two
(Deep below the sea)

THE MAGNIFICENT CASTLE of King Enahs shone with much brightness across the ocean Kingdom. The much glittering among the surrounding coral together with the gentle swaying colourful flowers of the anemone bushes had all kinds of sea-creatures frolicking among this coral and the many anemones.

It was this merriment of his sea creatures a short distance from the rainbow reflected castle that had King Enahs swimming happily with the beautiful mermaids, Lorac and Lyreb. Knowing Lyreb, the old water witch's daughter to be more beautiful than Lorac, his believing beauty was in the beholder, King Enahs's hearts' desire had chosen Lorac.

Deep down in his heart King Enahs knew how much he loved Lorac and so it was that he asked her, "Will my beautiful mermaid, Lorac, marry her King?" The king had always wanted the lovely Lorac for his queen, to rule beside him forever.

Lorac's happiness at King Enash's proposal, had her happily answer, "If that is my King's desire, then this mere mermaid accepts!" And so it was, King Enahs and the mermaid Lorac became betrothed.

Lyreb was happy for her king and her true friend Lorac and spoke sincerely, "May you both be truly happy."

Enfolding Lyreb to her, Lorac answered, "You are my true friend and you will be beside me when the king and I wed."

It was when the old water witch heard of the King's choice of a bride that she became angered to a great fury. Lyreb was her only daughter and her most treasured possession and the King had chosen another for his bride. The fury she felt for King Enahs and Lorac had her plunging from her cave. With her ugly pet serpent Sazoone clinging tight to her back she skimmed wildly through the waters. Her furious thrashing of her stunted tail had Sazoone clinging tighter to her.

Swirling wild in circles stirring the smooth waters into heavy froth the water witch's shrieking echoed eerily across the ocean floor, "How dare the King insult me by not choosing my beautiful Lyreb for his queen!"

Seeing Enahs floating happily with Lorac and Lyreb, the old water witch stopped her wild spinning and floated towards the three mer-people. Stopping in front of the startled three she stiffly pointed her long gnarled finger accusing at Enahs.

Recognising her mother's evil glaring and knowing what evil lay behind the glare, Lyreb gasped, "Mother!"

Ignoring her daughter, the old water witch floated deliberate and menacing closer to Lorac and Enahs. Twisting her deformed body to a jerking stop she glared more evilly at Enahs as she shrieked, "You will marry your ugly mermaid! But! She will have no mer-child! And your kingdom will lose its glitter! Cackling loud and grabbing hard to Lyreb's wrist, pulling her startled daughter after her, the old water witch slithered eel-like away. Still clinging tight to the old water witch's back, her pet serpent, Sazoone switched his spiky red tongue spitefully out at Lyreb.

With her mother's tight hold on her wrist and needing all her speed to keep up with her mother's fast dashing through the water and thinking of her mother's horrible curse on the king and Lorac, Lyreb did not see the Sazoone's evil action.

Chapter Three
(King Enahs and Lorac's Wedding)

Some time passed since the old water witch's curse on Enah and Lorac. All the sea-creatures were happily preparing King Enahs' kingdom for the royal wedding. Mermaids and mermen cleaned already colourful coral with clumps of anemone leaves and long strands of seaweed. With other sea-creatures the sea-horses cleaned the sea bed. They giggled between themselves as they watched the octopus with his many tentacles cleaning everything in his sight. King Enahs' kingdom shone as never before.

Finally the Royal wedding day arrived!

Mermen attended to King Enahs, draping him with assorted green anemone leaves.

Lorac was being attended to by giggling mermaids, adorning her with soft flowing flower petals picked from the seaside of the sandy shore.

Seated majestically upon their thrones, King Enahs and Lorac were married by the old-mer-man-of-the-sea, Shaan Daan.

To celebrate the royal wedding all the sea-creatures sang merrily as they frolicked around their king and queen. The kingdom was a melee of much merriment.

The happy watching Lyreb, adorned beautifully in soft swaying sea flower petals smiled as the king kissed his bride. The joyous sounding shrills of; "Much happiness to our King and Queen!" had the merriment become louder.

... The shadow slowly approaching the castle had the merriment suddenly stopping. Alas! The old water witch's curse was becoming true. The kingdom was beginning to lose its sparkling glitter. Frightened by what was happening, mermaids, mer-men, sea-horses, fishes of all kinds and octopuses darted away.

Lorac looked sadly at Enash, "The curse has begun, my King."

Much time passed since King Enahs and Lorac's betrothal and for a long time after the Royal wedding and the darkening of King Enahs' glittering Kingdom that the sea-creatures lived in a time of dullness.

Having watched his subjects' sadness a long time, King Enahs summoned all the sea-creatures to the castle.

Seated beside her King, Queen Lorac listened as he spoke kindly to his subjects, "Our Kingdom can become once more a happy kingdom! Happiness is not of beauty alone! Happiness comes from within us! You all must believe your king when he tells you this!"

The sea-creatures not believing their king began their search to find this happiness. It was not long before King Enahs' dull Kingdom was again filled with much happiness.

Time passed peaceably but it was when queen Lorac became ill that the sea creatures began to worry. Many of the sea-creatures cried because they thought their Queen was dying. It was to the greatest joy of the kingdom that one of the old water witch's curses had not come true. Queen Lorac was with mer-child. Before Coral was born, Lorac suffered great sickness, but now, looking down at her mer-baby she felt much joy. There was great merriment to celebrate Coral's arrival.

Time passed and Coral grew into a pretty mer-child, loved by all the sea-creatures.

Queen Lorac's sickness returned and she excitedly told King Enahs, "My King! Your Queen is again with mer-child!"

The celebration of Dearra's birth was great. The old water witch's curse again failed. Dearra grew to be more beautiful of the sea creatures.

The old water witch was much aware of the two mer-babies. When first hearing of the mer-baby Coral, she had not known such a fury. So angered that her curse had failed she screeched long and eerily, "What evil spell has dared to defy my curse?" Calming her rage, she told Sazoone, "I will ignore this ugly mer-baby." And so she did. But it was hearing of the second royal mer-baby that the old water witch went into an uncontrollable rage. Screaming at Sazoone, "You stupid serpent!" she lashed wildly out at him. Slashing his tongue out at her and so she could not touch him, Sazoone slid further down her back. She contented herself to watch the royal family from her cauldron.

The old water witch had known for a long time that there was a greater magic than her own and that her own magic could be taken from her. Not knowing if or when this other magic would destroy her, calming her fury, the old water witch hissed evilly to Sazoone, "Just like the other mer-baby I will ignore this ugly one. True to her word, the old water witch ignored Coral and Dearra and did not visit the castle.

Time passed and Coral and Dearra grew into kind and happy mermaids.

While Princess Lorac and her younger sister, Princess Dearra floated happily together, the old water witch had no need to visit King Enahs' castle. In her dark cave she and Sazoone watched the beautiful Princesses in her cauldron, Everything that happened in King Enahs's Kingdom was spied on by the old water witch. She watched jealously at Lorac and Dearra's happy frolicking, her evil cackling echoing within the rocks of her cave. "Do those stupid and ugly creatures think I do not see them? But I do see everything." Her hands rubbing heavily on her cauldron, she hissed, "You are my faithful mirror to all that lives in the sea and …" What the old crone now saw in her cauldron, had her disbelieving the vision. The vision she saw, was of her only son Kram grinning as he swam toward the laughing mermaids.

The vision the old water witch saw, was her only son, the handsome Kram, courting Princess Dearra. Seeing the two together, she forced the vision from her. Another vision of there being a more powerful magic than her own flashed quickly before her. With Sazoone clinging to her back and again in a fury, her rage greater than ever before and needing to visit King Enahs and Queen Coral's castle, she was swirling angrily through the calm waters. Her wild thrashing again caused the calm waters to form into into thick foam. Her head close to Sazoone's she screeched, "How dare they!" First the King spurns my Lyreb … and now their ugly Pincess, Dearra has put a spell of love on my Kram!"

Chapter Four
(Dearra's heart's desire)

THE SEA CREATURES knew the trembling of the ocean floor meant the old water witch was angry. Frightened mermaids and mermen hid behind thick coral and large rocks. Even the bravest of the sea-horses rushed to hide themselves. Fish of all sizes darted amongst the thick anemone and hollow coral stems. Crabs and octopuses burrowed deeper into the sand.

The tremors had King Enahs and Queen Coral worried as they swam from their castle in search for their daughters. They found Princess Coral comforting a group of young mer-people. Swimming hurriedly to Coral, Queen Lorac anxiously asked,

"Where is your sister Dearra? We must all be together to…"

A very frightened Dearra swimming to her mother's side, asked, "What is happening, Mother?"

Queen Coral was about to answer her youngest daughter when Kram swam swiftly between them. Putting his hand upon Dearra's shoulder, Kram whispered, "My precious mermaid! I will always be beside you to keep you safe. Queen Lorac had watched from afar, the love between the two young mer-people and Dearra's look of love towards Kram had not surprised her. Not knowing from where the young merman came, Lorac had happily accepted as a suitable husband for Dearra. It was with sudden thought of her faithful servant Tan that

Lorac began to look around for him. She saw him playfully teasing several small fish.

Tan felt had felt the tremor and knowing what it meant, he ordered the fish to scurry away to their homes. He had not noticed his King and Queen until the old water witch appeared angrily before them. Worried for his king and queen, his fear; for the first time, overcame his curiosity and he hid himself behind the large clump of coral. He wanted to hear what the old water witch was saying. Her screeching angry at his king and queen, trembling, he hid closer to the coral. Tan was not a brave servant and even if he were, he would be powerless against the spells of the old water witch. Tan knew he could only listen.

"With your evil daughter you have bewitched my only son, Kram ! For this deed you will be vanished to the deepest and darkest of the ocean. You and your Queen will rule in the darkest Kingdom! Waving her outstretched hands angrily at Enahs and Lorac, she added, "You will never return until my spell is broken!"

Tan watched helpless and terrified as the old water witch swirled heavy and fast around his king and queen. The strong whirlpool lifted Enahs and Lorac high above the palace. The old water witch's shrill cackling echoed across the kingdom. As the waters become calm, King Enahs and Queen Lorac were nowhere to be seen.

Satisfied her curse was done; the old water witch ceased her cackling.

Sobbing for the loss of their parents, Carol and Dearra clung to each other as Kram stayed close to them.

Sazoone slid his spiked tongue out at the three mer-creatures.

Turning to the sobbing mermaids, the old water witch pointing her finger accusing at Coral, began her curse, "You will be cursed forever! But unlike my curse on the Queen … your mother … there will never be a mer-child for you! My curse for you is true and it is now done!" Facing the trembling Dearra, the old water witch hissed, "I have a special curse for you, most beautiful of all mermaids!" Her spiteful laughter had Kram pulling Dearra close to him as he pleaded, "Please!

Mother! Do not continue with this evil!" Holdng Dearra closer to him, he continued his pleading, "Mother! I love Dearra. I have chosen her for my bride and…"

The old water witch screamed, "Aaahhhhh! Your bride! She will be no bride!"

Almost choking with rage and her chanting begun she cruelly pulled Dearra from Kram's arms. "You be changed into an old crone, forever!

Nooo! Mother! Do not do this evil thing!" Grabbing for Dearra, Kram caught several strands of her yellow hair. But he was too late to save his beloved, mermaid.

Terrified by the old water witch's mirthless cackling Dearra swam from the castle.

Swimming fast to reach his princess, Tan floating in front of her, asked, "Can I help you, Princess Dearra!" He was shocked as he watched his princess turn into an old crone. Her deep cackling, "Be away with you merman before I turn you into a fish … a teeny fish." caused him to float slightly from her. Giving an evil laugh she glided swiftly away … but not before Tan saw the streaks of yellow hair at the back of her head. In the long times to come, Tan would often wonder about the golden strands. Why were they not a tangled mess like the rest of the old crone's hair?

Deep in his thoughts, Tan was startled by the old water witch's scream causing him to look around. He gave a long gasp as he saw the old water witch change her son, Kram into a larger-than-large bloated John Dory. A hungry fish that ate a lot.

Swimming around in circles, Tan knew he had to hide … and quickly. It was from behind the thick anemone clumps he watched the old water witch slithering and cackling amused around something he could not see. His curiosity to see what the old water witch was cackling at and hoping to hear what she was saying, caused Tan to become careless as he swam from the anemones and float closer. He was surprised to see Princess Dearra once more as the beautiful mermaid. He heard the old water witch warning her, "Listen well pretty mermaid for it will not be spoken of again! Dearra saw Tan floating closer and with her eyes made signs at him.

Thinking the princess was putting a spell on him, Tan watched fearful. He need not have alarmed himself. Dearra was warning him to stay hidden. His chest heaving he floated to the large Coral stem and darted behind it.

Glaring at Dearra as she weaved her fingers evilly the old water witch cursed, "My spells and curses can only be broken by one other who must be part of the sea! Such a one would be a dark-haired mermaid and as loving as yourself. Your sister, Queen Coral will become her mother. This mermaid will give to you; as the old crone; a kiss felt from her heart. She will also; for a much greater love; cut off her hair and give it to you. You must then sing your song of true love … it will only be then, and only then that my curses can be undone!"

It had been earlier when the old water witch had looked into her cauldron and saw; with much fear; a vision of the power of such a mermaid. The maiden, not being aware of her precious gift will have the power to change her; the old water witch; into the darkest stone and banish her to the murkiest of the ocean for eternity. Angered at the vision, she hissed evilly.

Pointing her finger at Dearra, the old water witch continued, "Queen Coral will never have such a mer-baby, and so my curses are done!"

Dearra turned once more into the old crone.

Giving the old crone a heavy push which sent her spinning fast through the water the old water witch screeched after her, "One thing more before my curses can be broken, your song must be of true love!" The old water witch new the old crone could never feel true love.

Having skulked behind the old water witch's back, Sazoone now pushed his head against her scaly face.

The dark shadow stopping above Tan had him trembling.

Pushing a gnarl finger at Tan, the old water witch hissed, "You have heard much! So..oo.ooo! I will be putting a curse on you also, merman!

Recalling what the old water witch did to her Kram, Tan, finding a strength he did not know he possessed, swam swiftly under the far off rock ledge.

With a loud cackle, the old water witch sneered, "You are a stupid merman! You cannot escape from my spells." Enjoying the look of fear in Tan's eyes the old water witch spoke threatening, "You now know the secret of how my curses can be broken so I be letting you live so you can suffer. If you speak of my curses to Princess Coral I will curse you both that you will die painfully, also the Princess Dearra." With Sazoone clinging to her back the old water witch quickly vanished.

For a long time after the old water witch had gone, Tan's body shook. Finally floating from under the rock Tan knew he should tell Princess Coral about the curses. He also knew that to keep his Princess safe from harm he must forever keep his secret inside him.

The bloated John Dory swam close to Tan but the Tan had no fear of the big fish. Craning his neck to look into the eyes of Kram, Tan told him, "Your beloved Dearra will return to you." As the John Dory started turning away, Tan believed he saw the fish blink.

Knowing the fate of him and the Princesses Coral and Dearra, Tan knew he would never reveal the old water witch's secret of her curses. With much sorrow in his heart he hurried to find Princess Coral.

Chapter Five

(Tan swims to the top of the ocean)

High above the ocean floor small waves, being tossed gently back and forth by a soft breeze, glittered as millions of diamonds under the bright sun. Stronger waves began tossing the small waves higher to scatter them like tiny jewels towards the clear blue sky. It was among this glitter that a lone merman swam.

Tan was not really brave but hearing earlier that several mermen and mermaids had swum to the top of the ocean he went in search of them. As frightened as he was of the fishermen and their boats Tan searched across the waves. His frowning look meant he had not yet found them. Knowing he must bring the mer-people back he kept searching. Giving a last nervous look across the waves and then up at the approaching dark clouds, Tan, about to dive saw the young rebels. Swimming over to them, he warned, "The next time you disobey the Queen's orders and if I must search for you again, I will inform your Queen!"

It was while Tan waited nervously for the last mermaid to dive under the waves that he saw the mer-baby on the large flower floating towards him. Hearing the far off voices of the fishermen, Tan panicked. Hurriedly he dived downwards, deeper and deeper beneath the waves until he reached the safety of King Trebor's kingdom. Tiring from his long dive downwards Tan was happy to see castle. Relief that he was safe and floating towards the castle, he admired the many pearls of every colour and size entwined around the shells and coral walls of the castle. Coloured coral grew close by and it was with each playful rippling wave that this coral cast its' brightness everywhere.

Although King Trebor's kingdom did not shine as brilliant as King Enahs and Queen Lorac's had, it did have a magical look.

Tan remembered the kindness of King Trebor. It had been soon after the Royal wedding that all the sea creatures were summoned to the castle. It was Queen Coral who told them, "Until the glitter has returned to your King and Queen's Kingdom you are to come live in King Trebor's kingdom!"

The sea-creatures applauded Queen Coral. And so it was that the sea-creatures lived once more in brightness.

Resting on some coral, Queen Coral was watching several mer-babies playing noisily. Smiling as she watched the mer-babies she thought of her heart's desire to have a mer-baby of her own. Giving a slight frown, she told herself, To have my dearest desire come true, I would be the happiest mermaid in all the Kingdoms. But Alas! Queen Coral knew this could never be. She tried not to show her sadness to her King, but King Trebor saw and knew the reason for his queen's sorrow.

Watching his Queen then seeing her smile turn a little sad, the king swam to her.

Putting her hand gently under Trebor's chin, Queen Coral sobbed softly, "My King, I know I have all that my heart desires and your Queen is grateful but there is something I desire most of all … a mer-baby for us both to love."

Knowing of the old water witch's curse that there would never be a mer-baby for them, kissing Coral on her forehead, Trebor hoped he could soon make his queen happy. He knew his queen would; for a short whil, be happy when she again visited her parents at the deepest and darkest of the kingdoms. King Trebor's greatest wish was that the old water witch would not find out about his Queen's visits.

BUT! The old water witch did know of the Queen's secret. In her cauldron, she saw everything. She gloated each time Queen Coral entered the gloomy castle. The old water witch gloated more as she watched Princess Dearra; in her moment of change from the old crone into the beautiful yellow-haired mermaid; enter the castle then shortly scurry out as she changed in the blink-of-an-eye back to the old crone. Knowing Dearra never remembered her visits to her mother and father, the old water witch cackled evilly.

Farewelling her king, Queen Coral continued watching the frolicking mer-babies.

"My Queen! My Queen! I have found her!"

Tan's excited voice had the queen toppling from the coral. Swimming to balance herself, she smiled as she asked, "What have you found Tan that is so important that you should frighten your queen so?"

Breathless and excited and momentarily unable to tell his Queen his wonderful news Tan pushed his long, shimmering tail upward.

Amused at Tan's nervousness, Queen Coral said, "Do be taking your time, Tan. Surely your news must be so important to you …"

Interrupting his Queen, Tan firmly stated, "But it is, my Queen! I have found her! I saw the mer-baby on a large flower!"

Not taken offence of Tan's interruption of her person, Queen Coral thinking her servant imagined what he just told her, teasingly she asked, "Then why did you not bring the mer-baby back with you?"

Nervously shaking his head, he stammered, "Because of the fishermen and their nets, I was afraid to stay … they might have caught me.ee.e!"

"Do not fret my faithful servant. Your news pleases me. I will go in search of this mer-baby myself and…"

Again Tan interrupting, "No! No! Your majesty must not go alone!"

Smiling at Tan, Coral spoke gently, "Then you must come and keep your Queen safe." Watching the surprised Tan, Coral asked, "Will you come with me to protect your Queen?"

Knowing his Queen could not go alone; Tan hesitated before answering, "If that is my Queen's command."

Seeing Tan's hesitation, Coral spoke regally, "You have spoken like a true and loyal subject Tan. Thank you for offering to come with your Queen." Accepting Tan's slight nod as his answer, Coral swam ahead. o

Swimming continuously behind his Queen, Tan saw his queen was tiring but he also saw her excitement.

Unaware of her hard swimming Coral was thinking about the mer-baby, If she were not of the sea but of the humans, she would wait near the shore until a human came to rescue the mer-baby. Almost to the top of the ocean Coral called to Tan, "Are we there?"

Swimming to his queen's side; they both floated just below the waves, Tan assured her, "Yes! My Queen!" The dark shadow above their heads had Tan pointing as he called out a warning, "LOOK!"

Grabbing hold of Tan's arm, Coral waved her other hand in warning, "We must be careful … it could be the humans."

Realising the size of the shadow, Tan answered, "It is too small to be a human's boat." Braving a look above the roughening waves Tan, looked around him and then swam quickly and excitedly back to his queen. "It is the mer-baby! She is still there!"

Realising that Tan could not be persuaded to go above the waves again, Coral herself was becoming slightly afraid. Waving to Tan to stay under the waves, his relieved expression had her forgetting her own fear as she thought, Poor frightened Tan. He will never change. But I love him for who he is … my dear friend and faithful servant.

Chapter Six
(Queen Coral felt something pulling on her tail)

Darting heavily above the high waves Queen Coral was not a moment too soon. Distracted with finding the mer-baby Queen Coral was startled as the large fish swimming heavily towards the mer-baby flipped the flower over toppling the black-haired mer-baby into the waves. Looking in horror as the fish looked hungrily at the flower Queen Coral was hoping the fish had not noticed the mer-baby floating on the low wave. To Coral's relief the fish was only having a yawn. She had not at first recognised old Tinker. He had grown quiet large and apparently lazy. Queen Coral knew if Tinker swam too many times above the ocean the fishermen would catch him in their nets.

Diving shallowly Queen Coral came up under the tumbling mer-baby. Grabbing the mer-baby to her she saw she was of the sea. At this discovery Coral felt much happiness as she whispered, "I am truly the happiest of all mermaids.

Realising she had lost her direction; Coral began searching anxiously about her. She was wishing that her faithful servant Tan was with her … but she knew he was waiting under the waves. Having lost all direction of which way she was to swim, Queen Coral felt something pulling at her tail. The sudden appearance of Tan, startling her, she did not let go of the mer-baby.

Worried for his Queen's safety and overcoming his own fear he first pulled at his queen's tail and than surfaced beside her to lead her back under the now fierce waves. "Come! My Queen! We must hurry away!"

Her arms firm around the mer-baby, Coral dived gracefully downward. Tears of joy trickled down her cheeks to flow in the calming waters.

As they dived and floated down and down, Tan and his queen shared the carrying of the mer-baby. As they came in sight of the castle, it was Queen Coral who held the now sleeping mer-baby.

Wanting to know what their queen had found, many sea-creatures swam nearer. They all in turn praised the mer-baby's beauty … but seeing her black hair they swam slightly from their Queen.

It being a long time since the mer-creatures had seen their Queen so happy, the sea creatures hoped their queen's happiness was not one made of the old water witch's curses. Because of this tiny mer-baby gift, their Queen's beauty shone as never before. Overcoming their fear of the black hair, the sea creatures lingered closer to admire the mer-baby.

Worried for the absence of his Queen and now seeing her, King Trebor began floating towards the group of mer-creatures. He suddenly stopped floating when he saw his Queen coming towards him. "Where have you been, my Queen? I have been searching a long while for you!"

Tan floated beside his queen. Knowing his Queen would want to be alone with her King and the mer-baby he swam swiftly away.

The King, his hand on Coral's arm, asked, "What have you there?"

Giving a slight giggle, said, "It is a mer-baby my King. I …!"

Interrupting his queen, Trebor teased, "I know it is a mer-baby … but to whom does she belong?"

Without answering Carol passed the sleeping mer-baby to him, tears again trickled down her cheeks to mingle with the calm waters.

Holding the mer-baby close Trebor asked, "Why is my Queen crying?

Passing the mer-baby back to his queen, Trebor put his hand on Carol's.

Smiling up at him, Coral sobbed, "Trebor! I am so happy. We now have a mer-baby of our own to love!"

The Royal couple enjoyed their moment of great joy. It was King Trebor who broke the spell as he asked, "What shall we call her."

Giving a short laugh, Coral answered, "Would you like to choose a name?" Delighted at being chosen to name the beautiful mer-baby, Trebor began teasing his queen by pretending to not know any names. "Bel … no? Mar …no?"

Gently pushing at King Trebor's hand, Queen Coral laughed, "Do not tease me, my King."

As the mer-baby opened her eyes and gurgled, Trebor stopped his teasing. Kissing the mer-baby on her forehead, he told the mer-baby, "You will forever be known as Katina." Passing the smiling mer-baby back to his Queen he waved as he swam away.

Queen Coral was overjoyed when discovering the mer-baby was of the sea and she and Trebor now had their own mer-baby to love. She truly liked King Trebor's name, Katina.

Chapter Seven
(The sea world accepts Katina)

Katina grew into a mischievous mer-child whom all the sea-creatures adored. And so … King Trebor's kingdom became more happier.

Looking into her cauldron and seeing the happiness in the Kingdom and not liking what she saw, the old water witch became angered to such a rage that her rage sent the cauldron shaking and the water frothy. Two of my curses have failed … and now … the ugly queen has found an ugly mer-baby!" Her face close to Sazoone's, cackling, she screeched, "I will put a curse on the mer-child that will make the Queen so unhappy, she will never smile again!" Twisting wildly about her cave, the old water witch began scheming of a very evil curse to put on Katina.

The shaking of the ocean had Queen Coral look around from watching Katina and her friend Marla frolicking around some coral. "I wonder what evil the old water witch is brewing up now." Too happy to dwell on one so evil, Queen Coral smiled at her daughter as she softly spoke, "You both will soon be strong enough to swim through the largest of the coral." Scooping Katina into her arms and kissing her cheek, Queen Coral said, "Say goodbye to Marla for we must be welcoming your father home from his journey back from the shipwreck. The King has promised his little mer-child a surprise."

Wriggling from her mother's arms and then holding her mother's hand, Katina began swimming excitedly beside her. They did not have to swim far. The king, his large tail thrashing furiously, greeted them with a wave of his shining hand then glided gently to them. The jewels in his hand almost blinding, Katina let go of her mother's hand. To let Katina's eyes accept the brightness of the jewels the queen swam between Trebor and Katina. Quickly hiding his hands behind him, he greeted them, "Hello my pretty mermaids! I have a gift for each of you." Bringing his right hand into view and holding the necklace of many coloured pearls out to Coral, kissing her on her forehead, gave the necklace to her. Queen Coral returning his kiss thanked him.

"For you my daughter, it being your Birthday, I have a special gift."

Giggling excitedly, Katina swam quickly to her father causing him to bring his arm forward. Katina again almost blinded by the bright glitter.

Bringing the small necklace into view and waiting for Katina to get accustomed to the glare, the king then placed the necklace over her head.

To the King and Queen's surprise Katina's small body began to sink... down ... down ... The necklace dragging her further down it was with much fear Katina screamed, "Mother!"

Together the king and queen dived after their daughter. Grabbing hold of each arm of the frightened Katina, they stopped her fall. King Trebor holding Katina close to him, whispered, "You will become used to your necklace."

Witnessing the King's rescue of his daughter, the old water witch's piercing scream echoed across the sea bed. Her spell on the mer-child had not happened. "The mer-child was to fall fast and heavy to the rocks deep below, breaking her neck!" Furious that her spell had come undone, the old water witch glared hateful and long at the quivering cauldron.

Katina, safe in her father's arms, the Royal family swam happily back to the castle. Truly happy with her father's gift, Katina, with her mother's permission, swam off to find Martha and to show her shining necklace to her friend. While searching for Marla, Katina and her necklace was gazed upon by the sea-creatures.

Most of the sea-creatures knew why Katina looked different, with her long black-coloured hair and her slight shape in her body as though she were meant to have legs like the humans on the shore. No mermaid or merman told Katina how she was found floating on a large flower petal and brought down by their Queen to live with the king and queen as their own daughter. The sea-creatures knew, that when the time came, their Queen would tell Katina from where she came. It was out of Katina's hearing that the sea-creatures would say to each other, "Is not Katina the most beautiful and kindest of all mermaids?"

Innocent of the adored staring at her, Katina swam swiftly to find Marla. Seeing Marla frolicking with a baby octopus and two baby sea-horses, Katina called, "Hello! Marla!"

Smiling back at Katina, Marla greeted, "Hello Katina! What a pretty necklace" Lifting the necklace in her dainty hand and giggling at Katina, Marla said, "What a pretty necklace … and Happy Birthday, Katina."

"Thank you, Marla." Taking the necklace from around her neck, Katina giggling, said, "You must try my necklace on."

Green eyes open wide, Martha asked, "Can I truly wear it, Katina?"

"Just for a short while, then I must be going back to the castle." Katina having slipped the necklace over Marla's neck, both mermaids frolicked happily. Swimming with much melee over and under the coral and amongst the coloured anemone bushes, the mer-children were happy being together. Suddenly stopping their play, their small chests heaving, they promised never to leave each other but to remain friends forever.

It soon became time for Katina to go back to the castle, Marla returned the necklace.

"You can try my necklace on when again we meet."

Chapter Eight
(Katina asked, "Mother? Why am I not like other mermaids?")

OVER MUCH TIME, the old water witch tried many curses to destroy the royal sea-family, having them hated by all the sea-creatures. But to her great anger, her curses never seemed to be done and Katina still having birthdays would in time become a mature mermaid. The water witch being beyond reasoning put smaller curses on other mermaids.

Deep under the sea, special gifts were given for special occasions. The sea- creatures having heard the soundings of human voices above the sea drifting down through the waters about their special days called Birthday occasions,' and so it was that the sea-creatures liking these echoes, the echoes inspired the sea-creatures to give, on special times of the echoes, gifts for Birthdays to each other.

(The human beings who believed mermaids and mermen existed in the deep sea world, also believed that time was immortal. Not time, as in our human world where there is morning, afternoon, night, minutes and hours existing ... but under the sea where time seemed to be eternal.)

So it was that Katina continued sharing her Birthday gifts with her friend Marla. Marla, in turn, shared her Birthday gifts with Katina.

Over much time, Katina and Marla grew into young mermaids.

It was another birthday for Katina and she was excited to know what her present from her mother would be. She wanted to share her gift with Marla. Swimming swift and dainty through the many coral passages and seeing her mother watching her, Katina called, "Hello! Mother!"

Queen Coral swam swiftly to her daughter. Holding the sparkling bejewelled mirror out to Katina, Queen Coral said, "It is your birthday and this is your gift."

Holding the mirror, Katina gasped, "Mother! It is truly beautiful!"

Queen Coral watched amused as Katina swam happily in small circles looking at her reflection in the mirror. Katina had not seen herself properly and now she became aware of the gentle flowing of her long black hair. Turning to her mother, Katina asked, "Mother, why am I not like the other mermaids?"

"When you are older my young mermaid I will explain why but I must go now and welcome your father, the King." Having delayed explaining her daughter's question, the Queen left Katina to enjoy her birthday gift.

Seeing Marla waiting on some coral for her, Katina, just like her mother had done to her, hid the mirror behind her. Although Marla could not see the mirror she could see the sparkle. Happily playing Katina's game, Martha asked, "Where is your birthday gift Katina?"

Bringing the mirror from behind her, Katina held it up for Marla to take.

Looking in the mirror, Marla not having seen her reflection properly gave an excited cry as she asked Katina, "Is it truly me?"

Nodding, Katina answered, "It is truly you Marla."

Marla tiring of looking in the mirror and slightly annoyed at Katina's constant admiring herself, accused, "I am thinking you to be foolish!"

"Do you not like looking in my mirror, Marla?"

Still annoyed at Katina's vanity, Marla scoffed, "Not as much as you do, Katina!"

Placing the mirror where it would not float away, then resting beside Marla, Katina asked, "Are we still friends?"

Taking hold of Katina's hand, Marla said, "Forever friends."

Both mermaids were happy to see Scott, the young octopus and several mermaids floating towards them. The sea-creatures called, "A Happy birthday! Katina!"

The sight angering the old water witch, she swam from her cauldron.

Katina and Marla played games with Scott the octopus, and laughing mermaids. Around the swaying strands of kelp shrill laughter was heard. Small sea-creatures had joined in the merriment. Scott, the young but strong octopus agreed to let Marla and Katina with the other mermaids hold onto his long tentacles and he would twirl them around. Scott twirled slowly and then his twirling became faster … and faster. It was one by one giggling mermaids and sea-creatures loosening their hold to tumble into shimmering balls of yellow and green.

Small fish joining the melee swam in circles while mermaids swam onto the backs of bigger fish to ride happily up and down and over the coral and anemone bushes. But! As it was with all good fun, the playing had to come to an end … that was … until they met again and their merriment would start over again. Ripples swished around the mermaids as they swam away.

Scott had stayed a while longer to play. Soon it was time for Scott to leave the two giggling mermaids. Swirling through the rippling waves, he called, "I be seeing yee again, Katina and Marla."

Waving to Scott, the mermaids called after him, "Goodbye, Scotty!"

Katina turned to Marla and asked, "Marla! Are you happy? Have you ever wished to go to the top of the ocean?"

"Why would I want to get caught in a fisherman's net when I am happy here?"

Katina persisting, asked, "Would you not like to see a human?"

"No I would not!" Marla scolded then added, "Why would I want to look upon a cruel human?" Her hand on Katina's arm, Marla continued, "You should be happy living …"

Giving her tail a defiant thrash, Katina rudely interrupted Marla, "Well I would like to see a human! … And I will!"

Floating to Katina Martha said, "You must not think of such things!"

"I know it is wrong Marla and I do not know why but I do want to. I have tried not to talk about the humans, but I truly want to see one."

For a long time Katina had been thinking about the top of the ocean. She wanted with all her heart to look upon a human. The bad stories she had listened to about the humans only excited her curiosity. Having no idea of what a net was only that they were dangerous to all sea-creatures. Kissing Marla on her cheek, Katina asked, "Are we still friends?"

Crossing her small chest, Marla shyly answered, "Forever and ever."

Happily the mermaids pushed each other gently with their tails.

Katina knew it was not the time to tell Marla about her decision to go to the top of the ocean … but she wanted to tell someone. Katina knew she could trust Marla not to tel. Were they not friends for ever and ever?" Floating close to Marla, Katina told her, "Marla! I am going to go and see the humans!"

"No! Katina! You will be caught in their nets!" defiantly Marla added, "You are only a young mermaid and must not swim far from the Royal castle." Marla hoped Katina was only teasing her of going to the top of the ocean.

Seeing Martha's sad look, Katina smiled as she said, "Maybe one day I will see a human but for now, let us be friends forever and ever."

Marla's answer was almost a whisper, "Yes! Katina!"

Chapter Nine

("Why is my mermaid looking so sad")

Again much time passed ... Katina was resting on a piece of pearl entwined coral. Having playfully chased after Scott the octopus and his two octopus friends, she wanted to rest. She needed to think.

"Why is my young mermaid looking so sad?"

Not having felt her mother's presence and being surprised as to why her mother had come to her, Katina awkwardly slipped from the coral.

Pulling her sad looking daughter to her, Queen Coral asked, "Why is my young mermaid looking so sad? Does she not have all that her heart desires?" At her own words, Queen Coral's memories went back to not so long ago when just before the mer-baby had been found at the top of the ocean, the same words were spoken to her by Trebor, her King.

"Oh! Mother! What am I to do? I feel it is my heart's desire to see a human!" Katina wanted so dearly to see the wide ocean that her Uncle Tan had warned her about. The Queen's shocked look had Katina pleading, "Mother! Just let me have one look above the sea!"

Hugging Katina to her, a lone tear fell down her cheek. "I am truly sorry Katina. You are too young to go to the top of the ocean." Seeing Katina about to interrupt, Queen Coral spoke firm, "My word is final!"

Knowing she could not change her mother's mind, Katina sulkily answered, "Yes Mother."

Holding Katina's slim hands, Queen Coral said, "I tell you no my Princess, because you must understand how dangerous the top of the ocean is for us."

Not wanting to understand, Katina smiled at her mother as she answered, "I do understand your concern, Mother ... truly I do."

Believing the moment to soon be forgotten, Queen Coral also knew the young Katina was as curious as she was beautiful. Relenting in her decision, hugging and then kissing her daughter, the Queen chided, "If I take you to the top of the ocean to let you see a human, you must promise never to speak of them again to me."

"I promise never to speak of the humans to you again Mother, ever!"

Queen Coral whispered, "We must not tell of this to anyone."

Katina swam happily around her mother.

Swimming towards the castle, Coral said, "Before the sea-creatures awake, I will take you to see a human." Putting a warning finger to her lips and hoping she would be able to change her daughter's mind, the queen continued, "My young Katina, it is truly a long way ... and you are only a small mermaid and might not be able to finish your swim."

"I am only a young mermaid, Mother, but I can swim fast and long." Hugging her mother, Katina whispered, "Thank you, Mother."

Loving Katrina, Queen Coral's thoughts became troubled. Her heart would truly die if her young mermaid should ever leave her. Scolding herself for her thoughts, she smiled at her other thought that Katina being only a young mermaid and could not venture far from the castle.

Katina's excited thoughts of seeing a real human had her not noticing her mother's sadness.

Taking hold of Katina's hand, Queen Coral said, "Come, Katina, let us now go and welcome home our King.

Swimming happily, mother and daughter left behind them in

their wake, small rippling waves that flowed outward forming into the shape of a large flower.

It was in the quiet and stillness of the castle that the queen and her daughter began their early secret swim. They swam hard and long and Queen Coral began tiring.

Katina had swum far ahead of her mother. Queen Coral looking anxiously around saw the fast swimming mermaid and knew she had been foolish for not watching her daughter more closely. Queen Coral sternly called, "Come back Katina!"

Hearing her mother's command, Katina slowly swam back to her mother. For the rest of their swim, the queen swam close beside Katina.

They were almost to the top of the ocean when Queen Carol cautioned to Katina, "You stay here. I must be sure all is safe. A short while later and to Katina's relief she saw her mother diving down to her. "All is well, my young mermaid."

Mother and daughter surfaced together. Queen Coral wanted the waves to be rough so they could not continue. She had been disappointed when they surfaced. Gentle waves caressed their flowing hair. She had wanted the waves to crash loud and high to frighten her daughter and they would swim back to the castle.

Not knowing her mother's worried thoughts, Katina swam happily in wide circles.

Swimming swiftly and pulling Katina under the waves, Queen Coral gave her reckless mermaid a warning, "We must stay close to each other so we are not discovered!" The sudden shadow dwarfing them had the queen scream a further warning, "Dive further my young mermaid!" Queen Carol dived but soon realised Katina was not with her.

Emerging above the waves she saw her daughter swimming towards the boat. In fear she called, No! No! Katina! Come quickly!"

Ignoring her mother's warning and as she swam towards the boat, Katina called, "Look Mother! It is a human!" To Katina's surprise she was suddenly being pulled below the waves.

Having watched terrified at her disobedient daughter, Queen

Coral had swam fast to reach her reckless daughter. The queen did not let go of Katina's tail until they were deep under the waves.

Thinking she was in no danger, Katina wailed, "Mother! Please let me go!" But the queen kept her hold on her young mermaid.

Just as the sea world was beginning to stir, Queen Coral and Katina arrived back at the castle. Before the queen left Katina to play with her friends, she reminded her daughter of her promise, "You must tell no one about our swim to the top of the ocean"

Crossing her small chest with a dainty hand, Katina answered, "Our swim will be our special secret, and I will never speak of the humans to you, ever again, Mother"

Kissing Katina on the forehead, the Queen swam swiftly into the castle.

Chapter Ten
(Remembering it was Marla's birthday)

KATINA DARTING INSIDE the castle to collect her Birthday gift for Marla hurried to join the other mermaids. Hearing the happy melee, Katina knew Marla's party had begun. Marla's gifts were beautiful and plentiful. It was the necklace Katina had placed over her head Marla adored the most. Smiling down at the pearl necklace as she twisted it up and down shyly looked at Katina, "Thank you Katina. I will treasure your gift forever."

The melee subsiding, the mermaids having swum to their homes, Marla and Katina were left alone. Having watched Marla's happiness, Katina asked her, "Marla? Have you ever wanted to be something other than a mermaid, such as … a human?"

"Katina! You promised to never speak of the humans again …!"

Interrupting Marla, Katina pouting, said, "I promised Mother … and you are the only one to know of my heart's desire. … surely I can trust you Marla."

"You can trust me, Katina …"

Again interrupting Marla, Katina spoke excited, "Well ..ll.l! I will tell you! But you must promise never to speak of it to no one!"

Doubting whether she could keep Katina's secret, hesitating, Marla said, "I do not know if …"

"If you do not promise … I will not tell you!"

Flipping her tail and swimming a short way backwards, then floating in front of Marla, Katina asked, "Will you promise?"

Wanting to please Katina, giving a short nod, Marla said, "Alright, Katina! I promise!"

"I am going to the top of the ocean."

"But you cannot! You promised the queen!"

"I promised mother I would never speak of the humans to her." Teasing Marla, Katina continued, "It is different, my telling you …"

It was Marla's turn to interrupt Katina and she angrily told her, "There is no difference, Katina!

And you do know right from wrong and you are being selfish!" Speaking quieter, Marla asked,

"What if the humans should catch you?" Grabbing hold of Katina's arm, Marla almost sobbing, pleaded, "If ever the Queen should lose her mermaid, she would again be lonely and sad."

"I will come back, Marla! But if I should not, you can break your promise and tell the Queen."

To herself, Katina thought, Why should I not come back?

A short time passed and Katina was happy swimming with her mother as they again welcomed her father back to the castle. Although Katina played her mischievous games with her king and queen, Katina's longing to swim to the top of the ocean was becoming stronger.

Watching Katina tease her father, the king, Queen Coral thought, I love you so dearly my precious mermaid. Katina stopped her teasing of her father then swam quickly to the Queen and hugged her.

Not surprised at Katina's affection to her, Queen Coral asked, "My mermaid Princess is very loving today. What mischief have you been doing?"

With her small arms around her mother's neck and giggling, Katina then laughed, "None, Mother!"

Swiftly swimming ahead of the king and queen, Katina called, "I love you Mother and Father!"

The ocean bed was calm as Katina swam quickly from the silence of the coral adorned castle.

Not having told her mother of her intended swim to the top of the ocean and again getting Marla's promise to keep her secret, Katina hoped her mother would forgive her on her return. Of course Katina knew she would be punished for disobeying her mother and leaving the castle … and rightly she should be punished!

Swishing and twirling her colourful tail Katina swam up towards the brighter water. Beginning to get tired the young mermaid stopped her slow swimming and swished her tail slowly to keep her floating. Katina began to think about Marla's words, "You are too young to swim to the top of the ocean, Katina! You will become tired and start sinking and if you sink too fast … you could damage your gills and die. Oh please, Katina, do not do this foolish thing." Katina told herself, "Perhaps I should listen to Marla's warning and go back. Having rested many times, it was the rippling water deliberately pushing gently against her body that Katina felt she should continue her swim upward. Feeling the light chill of the water, Katina knew she had almost reached the top of the ocean. Surfacing amongst the gentle waves, her small body moving in rhythm with the gently flowing waters she felt a little frightened. Her soft but high-pitch voice as she exclaimed, "Everything is so..oo.o big!" had been heard by a small school of fish. Swimming over to Katina, the fish greeted, "Hello! What kind of fish are you?"

Her fear forgotten, Katina roused, "How rude of you to ask such a thing! I am a Royal mermaid!"

Swimming close to Katina and then bowing their heads mockingly at her, the fish chided, "Sorry your Royalness!" The melee of the fish as they honoured Katina attracted more fish.

Katina became frightened when the very large fish floated towards her. Beginning to sob, Katina thought, I should never have left the safety of the castle.

With his mouth open wide the large fish swam straight towards Katina. Thinking the fish intended eating her, Katina closed her eyes and waited to be eaten.

As the John Dory came within reach of Katina, the small fish screamed, "No…oo.o! John Dory! Stop!" Suddenly the evil and hungry look on the large fish suddenly vanished. It was the now grinning John Dory looking puzzled at the worried faces of the sea-creatures wondered what he had done wrong. Looking innocent at the glaring fish, he asked, "Why are you looking at me like that?"

The small see-through fish, swimming close to the big fish and pointing her fin angrily at him, roused, "John Dory! What ever came over you?" Swimming to Katina the fish again roused, "She is but a small mermaid! You should be ashamed of yourself!"

Seeing Katina open her eyes and begin sobbing, the larger-than-large fish said, "I do not know what made me act so badly Shelley or why…"

Chapter Eleven

BELOW THE OCEAN in the old water witch's cave the old water which darted angrily from her cauldron. Her curse had again failed. Her face close to Sazoone's spiky head, she cackled, "I will find a curse to destroy you, you ugly mermaid!" With Sazoone clinging to her back, the old water witch darted angrily from her cave.

All the sea-creatures began stirring and feeling the shaking of the ocean floor they knew that the old water witch was again angry. Unaware of why the water witch should be angry, the sea-creatures trembled at the thought that she might be coming for one of them!"

Back above the ocean, Shelley, the see-through fairy fish was looking accusing at the group of fish. She accused, "Look what your teasing of the small mermaid has done! It has frightened her."

One fish apologised, "We did not mean to frighten her. We only wanted to have fun." The other fish also apologised and so did, John Dory. "I do not know what came over me. Looking sadly at Katina, he asked, "Will you forgive me your Royalness." When Katina nodded, he hurriedly asked, "Do you want to play?"

Looking shyly up at the big fish and smiling, Katina said, "I would like to play a game, Dory."

And so it was that Katina and the fish frolicked happily among the waves and foamy froth. Katina was having so much fun with her new friends and not wanting their games to end, she called to John Dory, "Catch me!" Swishing her tail fast, she leapt onto the large fish's back then dived gracefully back into the foaming waves.

Diving deep, John Dory floated silently up behind Katina and grabbing several strands of her hair in his huge mouth bellowed, "I have caught you your Royalness!"

They had swimming races and each in turn won a race. Playfully clinging to Katina's tail with her fan-like fins, Shelley was having trouble hanging on as Katina thrashed her tail. Shelley toppling off, rolled into a rainbow coloured ball. Tiring of their games the fish asked Katina to tell them about her pretty castle and she did and she invited them to visit her. The fish in turn told Katina about the many places in their world and some of the places sounded frightening to Katina.

Excitedly Dory told Katina of a place where lots of ships had been wrecked and of the glittering things inside them.

Katina laughed at Dory's description, and then said, "Oh! John Dory! Do you not know anything? Those glittering things are called pearls and diamonds, just like my own necklace."

Feeling her neck for her father's gift to her, and finding it gone, she felt saddened at the thought she had lost it. Suddenly remembering about her earlier thought that the necklace would drag her down before she could reach the top of the ocean, she had left the necklace on her coral wall back at the castle. Smiling at the large fish, she promised, 'I will show you my necklace when we again meet.

The sea suddenly becoming rough caused many of the fish to swim hurriedly under the waves. Shelley spoke cheerfully, "We must b going now, but we will meet again Your Highness. We will play more games." And so, one by one all the fish left. Only John Dory stayed. Katina asked him, "Do you not have to go home, Dory?"

"I swim where ever and whenever I please, your Royalness."

"I must also be leaving you now Dory for I must hurry back to the castle before Mother is aware that I am missing."

"You swim swift and safe your Royalness."

"Goodbye for now, Dory! You beware of the fishermen's nets!"

As Dory swam away, he bellowed, "I will! Your Royalness!"

Chapter Twelve

(Marla will think me truly brave when I tell her I swam close to a boat)

To Katina, now alone, the sea seemed lonely and dark. She had not wanted the fish to go but she knew they could not stay. Realising she had not yet seen a human, Katina delayed her swim back to the castle.

The small wave encircling her had Katina gasp. The smoothness of the wave as it floated her through the water made the mermaid lose her fear. That was! Until Katina saw the wave was floating her towards the loan fishing boat moored just by the shore line.

The wave freeing Katina it then floated back among the bigger waves. The boat did not look frightening and as Katina floated closer to it, she thought, When I tell Marla how close I went to the fisherman's boat she will think me truly brave. The rippling waves tickling her tail, the giggling Katina swam closer to the side of the small boat. The young mermaid should have been listening to the soft swishing sounds … but when she did become aware of their swishing, Katina was too late!

The waves lifting the net, the net swirling loosely around in the quickening waves caught Katina. Struggling to free herself, Katina became more entangled. The frightened Katina suddenly becoming caught in the fisherman's net is terrified. Hoping Dory could still hear her, Katina called, Dory! … John Dory!" Knowing the big fish was now long gone, she called, "Mother! Please save your mermaid.

It was only the old water witch who saw and heard the frightened mermaid. Cackling to Sazoone, she spoke evilly, "Look long at the Princess my Sazoone! At last! The only one with power to destroy me! My curse has vanished her from the ocean."

In the darkness, Katina saw bright lights. She wondered if they were shining necklaces. Unable to free herself, she sobbed until she fell into an exhausted sleep.

Katina did not feel the rough waves or the several young fish trying to free her. Unable to free the mermaid, the fish had to leave her before they also were caught in the swirling net.

Time passing, Katina did not see the large yellow ball high above her or feel its heat. The sun became shadowed by the dark clouds changing to a fierce storm. Neither had she felt the cold chill breeze now blowing. Her body caught in the net Katina floated roughly beside the boat.

Several strands of her long black hair floating through the net seemed to be waving goodbye to the sea. Katina did not awaken.

Chapter Thirteen

It was early that morning when Tom, his shoulders slumped and heavily coughing and wheezing shuffled across the cold wet sand to his boat. He had not wanted to be out in such bitterly cold weather but he had to catch some fish. He was glad he had worn the jumper Katie knitted him and his thick Macintosh covering.

The other fishermen anxious to be netting their fish had rowed out to sea before day break.

Tom, not having slept well, Katie had let him sleep late that morning. Now reaching his boat he leant weekly on the side of it. Thinking about his bad luck, his catches lately not being many and the small amount of money he brought home and Katie never complaining, he pulled absently at his net. Not being well for many days, he had seen Katie's concerned looks towards him. He had tried hiding his pain from her, but Katie was not fooled. He knew Katie only agreed to him coming down to his boat this morning if he promised to wrap himself up warm. Tom still shivered. He thought of Katie's words as he left the house, "Tom, I do worry about you!" Smiling wanly his voice hoarse, he spoke low, "Katie can be quite bossy sometimes."

Pushing slowly from the side of his boat and gripping his net, his back aching, Tom began pulling at the loose net. Knowing the net was caught under the boat, pulled harder. The released net held four large fish. Pulling again to release the rest of the net, Tom stared amazed at the black haired girl. Thinking she was one of the neighbour's child and she had been caught in his net and drowned, he frantically pulled at the net. The coloured tail told him he had not; to his joy, found a human but a mermaid. Leaving the fish where they were, Tom stepped nearer the mermaid and grabbing her up in his arms had a closer look at her. His imagination and the drawings he had seen in books, had told him mermaids were so small with long yellow hair that you could hardly see them. Looking at the beautiful black-haired mermaid, almost as big as a baby human, Tom could not believe his eyes. He knew he must take her home to Katie. When Katina did not move and believing her to be dead, Tom stated sadly, "It is no use to take her to Katie. I must throw her back into the sea." The water being shallow and the thought of having to wade so far from the shore in his heavy boots, Tom told himself, "I will take her home just to let Katie look upon a real mermaid.

Katina's slippery body was making it hard for Tom to hold onto her as he trudged along the slippery sand. Grasping hold of several strands of Katina's hair he pushed Katina under his Macintosh. Hoping he would not meet anyone, Tom started stumbling across the wet sandy beach. He need not have worried about meeting anyone. The weather being too cold for the neighbours' children to play outside on the sand there was nobody else around to see the staggering, hunchbacked Tom with the shining tail and the black hair hanging below his Macintosh. Reaching his gate and seeing the worried Katie hurrying toward him he called, "Hurry Katie and open the door!" Tom's serious demand had Katie hurrying back up the steps and pushing the door open. Pushing past Katie, Tom again demanded, "Hurry and close the door, Katie!"

Curious as to what made Tom's coat bulge, Katie followed her staggering husband into the kitchen. Inside the kitchen, she asked, "Are you feeling more unwell, Tom?"

Opening his coat Tom put Katina on the kitchen table. Katie's loud gasp made him smile but remembering the mermaid was dead, his smile faded and he spoke sadly. "I think the mermaid is dead, Katie and ..."

Eyes wide with excitement, Katie interrupted, "Is she a true mermaid?" At Tom's nod Kati touched Katina's hair.

"Yes Katie … but she is dead."

"No! Tom! She can not be dead!" Sobbing, Katie said, "I want us to keep her John and love her as our own child!" Leaning over Katina, Kati begged, "Please little mermaid, open your eyes!"

"Bring wet cloths, Katie! We must keep her wet!"

Many hours Tom and Katie wiped Katina's lifeless body with the wet cloths, but to no avail. Katina had not showed signs of life. Refusing to give up on his mermaid, Tom hurried to the washroom. Bringing back their large round bathtub and while Katie kept Katina wet, he began filling the tub with water. Realising what Tom was doing, Katie left Katina and taking down a large jug from the cupboard, began helping Tom fill the tub. Tom put Katina in the tin tub.

Floating Katina in the tub, Tom and Katie watched for signs of life … but there was none. To the sobbing Katie, Tom whispered, "The mermaid was not meant for us, Katie." Looking at Katina's limp body, her tail spread open like a colourful fan, Tom said, "We must take the mermaid back to the shore so the waves can float her back to the sea.

"Looking at Katina, her black hair spread across the water, Katie asked, "Can we keep her for a short time longer, Tom? Just a short time so as we may look a while longer upon our mermaid's beauty?"

Giving Katie a sad grin, Tom nodded as he said, 'As we cannot take the mermaid back to the shore until it becomes dark, then we can…" Like Katie, Tom having also fallen in love with the mermaid, could not finish his words.

Katie had forced herself from looking at the mermaid to make a meal. Tom and Katie were not hungry and their meal was left untouched.

Knowing he could not delay taking the mermaid back to the shore, Tom told Katie, "I will walk to the shore and if there is no one there, I will come back for the mermaid." Tom's shuffling from the house to the shore had been reasonably quick but his return back to the house had become slower. It was Katie's excited calling as she ran from the house towards him that had Tom hurrying his shuffling. "What is the matter Katie?"

"Tom! Our little mermaid is alive!"

Wanting to believe Katie's words and hurrying to the kitchen door Tom stared in disbelief. Their little mermaid was truly alive. Her large blue eyes wide open as she floated contented in the tub.

When Katie lowered her hand into the water, Katina swam to it. "Look Tom! Our mermaid is not afraid of me!" Katie beckoned Tom to do the same. Katina stayed near Katie's hand. Giving a shaky laugh, Tom said, "Perhaps our mermaid does not like me." Katina suddenly floating to Tom held onto his fingers. Cautiously pulling Katina around the tub, Tom said, "I think our mermaid does like me now."

"She certainly does like you, Tom. Can we keep her?"

Katina said, "I am not afraid of you!" Not understanding the mermaid, her high-pitched voice had Tom and Katie push their hands to their ears.

Watching Katina for several seconds, Katie explained to Tom, "After you left I wrapped the mermaid in a towel and hugged her close to me and prayed. It was later Tom when I put her back into the water that I felt the feather-like touch of her hand on mine."

Without realising he was doing so, Tom waved to Katina. To his surprise, Katina waved back.

My Darling Katie I do believe we have ourselves not only a mermaid but also a child of our own to love. Beginning to get back his appetite, Tom told Katie, "I am feeling rather hungry Katie and …"

Before Tom could finish speaking, Katie answered, "So am I Tom.' Taking their cold meals from the table and as she re-heated them over the two saucepans of water, Katie called happily to Tom, "Is it not a miracle Tom that we now have the child we have always prayed for."

Katina had been with Tom and Katie for two months and John was finding he was not sick and his netting of fish was plentiful..

It was very early on a cool but sunny morning that Katie seeing

Tom dressed in his Macintosh, she asked, "Tom, should you be leaving so early?" Kissing Katie on her forehead, he replied happily, "Since our little mermaid came to us I have been better and my luck has changed. My catches have been many. Even the strange looking fish have sold well at the fish markets.

Tom's sea-catches had been plentiful and his change of luck had not gone unnoticed by the other fishermen. They jokingly asked him, "Have you found a mermaid?"

Telling them truthfully, Tom answered their questions, "I have found a black-haired mermaid!" to which the fishermen laughed at him. Tom did not let the fishermen's' taunts worry him. Tom had found it hard to believe at first that his mermaid had black hair and so he was pleased that his neighbours did not believe him. He did not have to explain about their mermaid.

He and Katie liked knowing they were the only ones who knew about their black haired mermaid.

Chapter Fourteen
(Mother … I know where Katina has gone!)

MEANWHILE … LIFE under the sea was sad. Realising Katina was missing Queen Coral had yearned sadly for a long while before summoning all the sea-creatures to search the ocean for her disobedient daughter. King Enahs searched the top of the ocean for his mermaid. Queen Coral, with many mermaids, searched the sea-bed for the missing Katina.

Not knowing Katina was missing but thinking Katina's long absence from their meeting place; was that Katina was upset with her; Marla had stayed far from the castle. It was not until the group of young mermaids and mer-men swimming close by Marla and talking about how all the sea-creatures were searching for Katina that Marla hurried home.

"Mother! Father!"

It was Marla's mother who told her daughter that her father had been summoned urgently to the castle. Seeing her husband swimming fast towards them, she called, "Samoht! Has Katina been found?" Shaking his head, Samoht called back, "Not yet! Ardnas!"

"Mother! I know where Katina has gone!" Marla realised too late that she had betrayed her friend. Breaking her promise to Katrina, Marla told her parents of her and Katina's secret.

Shocked at Marla's words, her parents hurried her to their Queen.

It was a frightened mermaid floating in front of the Queen who thought, Will the queen put a spell on me. Shaking and sobbing, Marla was afraid to look at her queen. Upset as Queen Coral was, she did not show her grief to Marla. Taking hold of Marla's shaking hand; she beckoned the upset mermaid to rest beside her on her throne.

"I did not know Katina had not returned. I thought she was angry with me and..."

Interrupting Marla, Queen Coral asked, "Why would Katina be angry with you,?"

"I..I...do not know my Queen. I thought she must have been angry with me when she had not come for a long time to play with me."

Much time passed before Queen Coral sadly abandoned her search for Katina. Realising her daughter was lost to her forever, thoughts of the fish nets and large fish caused her to tremble at Katina's fate. Her heart broken, Coral became again a sad queen to mourn for her lost mermaid.

Katina's necklace of pears and diamonds were left hanging from the pearl entwined coral wall. Her brightly coloured mirror and coral comb lay on her beautiful bed of coral.

Although much time had passed, Marla never forgot Katina. Had they not promised to be friends forever? Like the queen, Marla had cried a long time for Katina and had finally resigned herself to Katina's fate. To have Katina always near her, Marla always wore the pearl necklace, Katina's birthday present to her from so long ago.

Marla having grown into a matured siren, her singing entranced many mer-men and mermaids. Sea creatures would also swim to her side to listen to her melodious voice. Marla enjoyed singing for the sea-creatures but she became shy when seeing the handsome mer-man smiling at her. Watching the sea-creatures frolicking around her, Marla pretended not to have seen him; she would then swim swiftly away.

Ecnal watching Marla swim away, knew Marla saw him he then swam in the opposite direction. Knowing he loved the lovely mermaid,

Ecnal also knew Marla would be his and that he would wait for her. He did not have to wait long for Marla to learn of his feelings for her.

Giggling as she held her long flowing hair to her body Marla watched from behind her hiding place behind the wide piece of coral and as the merman swam out of sight, she knew she loved Ecnal with all her heart. Seeing the old merman swimming slowly past, Marla smiled, then waving, called, "Hello! Tan!"

Tan waving back, smiled wanly. He missed Princess Katina and seeing Marla, he was always reminded of the beautiful mermaid Princess. Knowing his Queen waited his presence at the castle, he hurried away.

Floating before his Queen, she invited him, "Come! Tan! Rest beside your Queen."

Looking questioning at the empty throne, Tan thought, Could I? A mere servant, dare?

Guessing Tan's hesitation, Queen Coral smiling, said, "Your King will not mind … my faithful Tan."

Doing as his Queen bid the old merman knew why his queen had summoned him. Although knowing his queen's question, he knew he would also have to ask his sad queen the same question.

"But Tan! I can not answer your question."

"And your faithful servant can not answer yours, my Queen."

"What is the meaning of your boldness to your Queen, Tan!?"

Bowing his head, Tan woefully stammered, "I do not intend to be bold my Queen.

I have been forbidden to reveal … oh please your majesty … do not ask your obedient servant to tell …"

Placing her hand on Tan's quivering arm to calm him, Coral spoke softly, "We will speak no more of the matter."

Having watched Queen Coral and Tan, the old water witch's deafening cackling as she floated evilly around her cauldron shook the cave walls. Darting closer to her cauldron and seeing the image of the old crone and the beautiful jewel encrusted shell attached to the large coral stem on the old crone's wall, mimicking Tan's voice the old water witch began chanting, "I know a secret that I am not allowed to tell! I …" Her cackling suddenly stilled. Some strange thing was happening. Her cauldron began to shake. The old water witch was seeing the old crone changing into the beautiful Dearra. The moment was short as Dearra changed quickly back into the old crone. Watching in her cauldron for a moment more she saw the old crone looking at the beautiful shell but not like the old water witch had watched, the old crone was able to touch the shell. As she touched the glowing shell she cackled, "You my precious hold a secret." As the glow of the shell faded and the old water witch's cauldron became calmed, the old water witch again cackled, "But first, much time must pass my mermaid!"

Having been blinded with rage at being reminded of the mermaid princess the old water witch did not see Queen Coral swim past her cave.

Queen Coral's heart, shattered by her grief and longing for the comfort of her parents, King Enahs and Queen Ahsram, the queen was swimming speedily to the darkest of the ocean.

Chapter Fifteen

("Katina! We must send you back to the ocean because …")

KATINA HAD LIVED with Tom and Katie for many happy years. Katina having gotten used to the human world, Katina was able to rest for short times on a chair. She also became used to the human food. She still had to eat salty seaweed and John collected the choicest pieces from the wettest-of-the-wet sand for her.

Having always kept to themselves, Katie and Tom never encouraged visits from their neighbours. Their neighbours' understanding of Katie and Tom being shy people they did not visit in their home; they did talk often to them from their flower bordered fences. Thus it was that Katie and Tom were able to keep Katina their secret. When a neighbour did chance to visit and Katie saw her coming up the garden path, Katie place Katina on a chair and wrapped a blanket around her.

Over the years Katie taught Katina to speak her language and of her human ways. Katina was soon teaching Katie her sea talk and telling Katie about her life under the ocean and of her mother, Queen Coral … and Marla and Tan and King Trebor's dulled castle, it having been cursed by the old water witch. Katina told Katie about her glittering necklace and pearl encrusted mirror.

Katie bought Katina a mother-of-pearl edged mirror and was surprised to see Katina always looking at her reflection. Watching the vain Katina, Katie needing to talk to Katina, said, "It is not proper that you keep admiring your reflection."

But Katina loved to look at her shiny black hair.

Many more years passed. Katie counting the years since finding Katina, said, "Today is your twelfth birthday Katina.

Katina loved Tom and Katie and had become more like a human. She told herself, "I am truly a human." Lifting her tail and fanning it wide, admired it. Smiling cheeky she said … "Well..ll.l! I am almost a human Katie. One day I will have legs like you and Uncle Tom!"

Hearing Katina's words began scrubbing at the apron. Katina starting to sing, Katie listened. Never had she heard such enchanting sounds. Leaving the apron soaking in the washtub, Katie stood at the kitchen door. As though being led by gentle hands towards Katina, Katie was almost beside the tub when Katina stopped singing. Almost falling as the spell was broken; Katie could not understand what had happened. Kneeling beside the tub, the entranced Katie said, "Katina! Your song was enchanting. So do sing another song.

Smiling as she held her mirror up to see herself, Katina sang softer and more melodious. Unexpectedly she began wailing loud. Her wailing was becoming eerie and frightening to Katie.

Katina loved Tom and Katie but she was missing her sea parents. Katina's sad singing became again soft but had again become high-pitched and Katie pressing her hand to Katina's mouth, said, "Please stop singing, Katina!" Katina stopped singing. Katie went back to her scrubbing. Katie told herself, I must tell Tom that Katina is missing her sea people.

Putting her hand under Katina's chin, Katie asked, "Why is my mermaid suddenly sad?" Katina wailed louder causing Katie to press her hands hard against her ears and yell above Katina's wailing, "You know Uncle Tom and I love you!"

Tom, seated at the table, the candle flame flickering large shadows around the room, he could not eat his favourite meal. Sitting sadly opposite her husband, Katie asked, "What shall we do Tom? I do not want to give our mermaid back to the sea."

"We must Dear Katie. We did know that one day Katina would leave us. … and we Katina's happiness must come first. We must let our mermaid choose for herself."

"But Tom … what if she wants to leave us and…?"

Placing his finger softly to Katie's lips, Tom interrupting sighed and then said, "We must be fair to our mermaid, Katie! I also do not want to loose Katina, but her happiness must come first." Grinning wanly at Katei, Tom added, "We must let Katina decide for herself."

"But! Tom! What if Katina truly chooses to leave us? "

"Let us wait and see, Katie." Standing up and seeing Katie about to argue, Tom walked to her and holding her close, whispered, "Everything will be alright."

Katie sobbed, "How can we let Katina go?"

Katina's thoughts as she rested against the side of the tub were of her mother and Marla. Tears brimming in Katina's eyes, she spoke aloud, "I wish I could see you again." Unaware of Katie and John watching her from the doorway, wiping a wet hand across her eyes, she softly sobs.

Walking silently over to Katina, Katie said, "We must send you back to the sea because…" Katie was unable to continue.

"Why send me back, Katie? You know I love you and Uncle Tom!"

"We believe it is best for you to go back to your own kind."

Her hands pleadingly outstretched towards them, Katina sobbed, "But Uncle Tom, I do not want to leave you and Aunty Katie." Placing her hand across her small chest, she said, "Something is hurting me here."

Katie and Tom, kneeling beside the tub took Katina's wet hand in their dry hands. Giving a low sigh, Katie tried to explain, "What you are feeling, Katina is love. Your heart is telling you how much you miss your sea world and so, when I go to my boat I will take you with me."

Hearing Katie's sobs, Katina spoke happily, "Do not cry, Katie. I promise to return to you and Tom." Smiling, Katina added, It may be some time before I return but I will come back to stay. And I will have two legs just like you and Uncle Tom."

Katina hugged Katie until her clothes were soaked. They both laughed.

Waiting until he knew the shore would be clear of the fishermen, Tom covered Katina in the thin blanket. The sad Katie walked beside Tom.

Tom carried Katina across the shore to the old low wooden pier. Gently placing Katina in the water Tom whispered, "Goodbye my treasure."

Katina waved to Katie and Tom and as the waves became higher, they carried Katina with them. Looking back toward the now distant wharf, waving sadly, Katie called, Goodbye Katina!"

As the sudden wave lifted Katina, she called back, "I will come back …wait for meee..ee.e!" The swiftness of the wave carried the mermaid towards the wide ocean.

Turning sadly to Tom, Katie said, "Our little mermaid has gone."

Nodding his head and taking hold of Katie' hand, they shuffled slowly back to their home.

Chapter Sixteen

(Marla? Does the old water witch and the old crone still live?)

THE DARK CLOUDS floating high above the ocean brought heavy splashes of rain but Katina did not notice as she rubbed at her eyes. The salty sea water was hurting them. Beginning to swim amongst the rough, deep waves Katina decided it was time for her to dive under the waves. Swimming down … down her eyes became again used to the salty sea. Her fish body seemed to become more grown up.

Passing the many and beautiful coloured coral reefs and the pretty swaying anemone bushes, Katina swam contented to the sea bed. Several small schools of fishes darted around her only to quickly vanish among the thickest anemones. Giggling as she glided through the clearing water she said, "Funny little fish."

Katina was recognising the different things and places when she heard, "Hello! Katina!" Many of the older sea creatures were calling to her. Recognising the old merman swimming slowly by, Katina called cheerfully, "Hello Uncle Tan!"

Keeping his slow swimming, he called back, "Hello little mermaid!'

Tan's greeting to her caused Katina to become sad as she thought, If Uncle Tan had forgotten her, then perhaps her mother and father had also forgotten her...

Tan's happy laughter interrupting her thoughts, she looked up to see Tan floating beside her. Staring at the Katina, he said, "It truly is our little lost mermaid comes back to us!" Taking hold of Katina's hand, Tan spoke excitedly, "The Queen will be ever so joyous!" Pulling Katina beside him he glided hurriedly towards the castle.

Her head bent low, Queen Coral watched the two small fish playing. So deep was the queen's watching of the two fish, she was not aware of Tan and Katina floating behind her.

"Hello Mother."

It had been so long since hearing her long-lost-daughter Queen Coral smiling looked up. Seeing nobody in front of her, her smile disappeared.

Giggling, Katina swam in front of her mother again, 'Hello Mother."

Queen Coral looked with disbelief at her daughter. Pulling Katina close to her, she gasped happily, "Katina! My little lost mermaid!"

Arms around her mother's neck, Katina said, "I am lost no more."

The love the two mer-people showed to each other was too much for Tan, and shedding tears of happiness, he swam from the happy scene.

Older sea-creatures welcomed Katina back, younger ones joining in.

Katina met many old fish friends and was glad they remembered her.

Finally alone with each other, Katina asked, "Mother! How is Marla?"

"Come! My beautiful and fully grown mermaid and see for yourself."

Close to the castle, surrounded by young mermaids and mermen, Marla, suddenly seeing Katina floating towards her, screeched, Katina! Is it truly you?" Hugging Katina for some time, both mermaids frolicked in and out of the anemones. Having talked for a long while, Queen Coral told Marla she must be going. "Off you go young mermaid, you will see Katina soon."

Following her mother into the castle Katina was surprised to see her necklace still hanging where she had left it. Swimming to the necklace and hurriedly putting it on she saw the beautiful mirror and coral comb the queen had also given her. It had been placed near

her necklace. Picking up the mirror and comb and remembering her favourite rock she glided from the castle. Swimming to her rock she sat a long while looking at the reflection as she entwined anemone flowers in her long wavy black hair. The sea-creatures were noticing that Katina was very different. She was vain about her hair and many sea-creatures began avoiding the once popular mermaid.

Although Martha found Katina's vanity upsetting, she stayed loyal to her friend. When Katina asked, "Marla, is my hair not truly lovely?" Marla would rouse, "Why must you always talk about you hair, Katina? It is no…"

Proudly Katina would interrupt Marla and state, "Well! Marla! My hair is more beautiful than all the mermaids! And I believe you are jealous." Turning angrily from Marla, her black hair flowing wide, Katina swam swiftly away. Hurt by Marla's words, Katina swam as fast and far from her friend. Her fast swimming had her suddenly stopping. Where was she? How far had she swum? Sobbing, she cried, "Oh Marla! I did not mean to argue with you." Looking around her, her anxiety turned to disbelief when she saw a dolphin swimming gracefully in circles. She saw high peaked, lavender tinted rocks, their peaks almost covered with white fluffy clouds. Floating slowly as she again looked around, she spoke aloud, "How did I swim so far?" The sudden movement beside her had Katina float slightly backward and seeing the beautiful fish, Katina asked, "Who are you?"

The grinning fish said, "Hello your Highness."

Recognising Shelley the fairy-like fish, Katina gasped, "Are you lost too, Shelley? … Are Dory and the others with you?" It was the sudden calling of "Surprise!" That had Katina giggling at the many fish creatures popping up from under the low waves and floating around her.

"Hello Dory!" She called to the larger-than-large fish. Dory called back, "Hello Your Royalness!"

Two pretty coloured dolphins swimming close to Katina, asked matter-of-face, "So! You are the beautiful Princess Katina?" The smallest dolphin introducing herself said, "I am called Eon and my sister is called Chance."

Frolicking with Shelley, Dory, Eon and Chance, in the wonderful rainbow colour world, the sea-creatures skimmed the gentle waves Dory made as he dashed past. Katina had not thought about her hair. Surrounded by the sea-creatures, Katina had to swim fast to keep up with them. Never having seen such beauty she did not want to leave the magical place. She swam a long while with Shelley and the others. Katina wanted to stay forever but knew she would have to leave her friends. Starting her swim towards the castle, she called, "Goodbye everyone…" The large wave lifting her up suddenly swept her far from the lagoon and Shelley.

Almost to the castle Katina saw Marla.

Expecting Katina not to be speaking to her and wanting them to still be friends, Marla had swum to the castle. Watching Katina as she swam swiftly towards her, Marla had to; in all honesty, agree with Katina that her hair was truly beautiful. But

Marla would not tell Katina. Katina was vain enough. Marla was surprised when Katina swam close and greeted happily, "Hello Marla! Do you want a race?"

The giggling mermaids swam a long while between large coloured anemone bushes and many wide holes of the pearl entwined coral reefs.

Katina's life under the sea was very happy. Although Katina's thoughts were often of Tom and Katie, she quickly settled into her life in the castle. Missing the Katie and Tom, she was becoming sad. She told herself, "I must go in search of Marla."

Marla was chasing several giggling mer-children when Katina swam in front of her. After the mer-children had swum swift and happily away, Katina asked, "Marla? Do the old water witch and old crone still live?"

"Yes! But why do you ask of one so ugly and evil who lives forever?"

"I do not believe the old crone is truly evil and I need her help." Suddenly giggling, Katina added, "But she truly is very ugly."

Martha angrily, "The old crone will not help none but herself, Katina!"

Proudly Katina stated, "I believe the old crone will grant me my heart's desire."

Seeing Katina's proud attitude and; because of her vain attitude, Marla wanted to hurt her friend. Marla accused, "And what is your heart's desire Katina? That your hair be even more beautiful than it is?"

"No! Marla! My heart's desire is to become a human to live with Uncle Tom and Katie forever in their cottage and have legs like them."

"You are being selfish, Katina! What of your mother the Queen and your father the King? Will you not think of their sorrow if you were to again leave them? …And what is a cottage?"

"I love my King and Queen, Marla, but my heart's desire is to become a human … and a cottage is what Uncle Tom and Katie live in."

"I do not understand what a cottage is but I do understand your heart's desire Katina. It is just that you are my friend and I do not want you to leave the sea."

"When I am human, we will still be friends forever, Marla."

"You promise, Katina?" Watching Katina cross her small chest, Marla hurriedly crossed her hands across her own chest.

Swimming swift behind Marla, Katina pulled Marla playfully by her tail. In turn, Marla pulled Katina's tail.

"I must be leaving you Marla." Seeing Marla's surprised look, giggling, Katina said, "I must be at the castle to greet the King and to let him know that his lost mermaid has returned."

"Waving to Marla and then as she started swimming away, Katina called, "I will see you!"

Marla called, "Goodbye for now, Katina!"

Chapter Seventeen
("No! Not my beautiful hair!")

Leaving the castle early, Katina swam in the direction of the old crone's cave. The closer Katina swam, the more nervous she became. The dark cave looked frightening among the dark green tangled bushes and brown coral. Stopping her swimming and beginning to float toward the evil looking cave Katina called, "Old Crone! Are you in there?" Looking around her and seeing no one in site, Katina floated more bravely to the dark entrance. Floating just inside the cave, she called, "Are you home! Old crone?"

The sudden appearance of the old crone and her cackling voice, "What do you want?" startling Katina, caused Katina to spread her tail fully out and float a short way backwards. Floating close, Katina stammered, "I wa…nt you to…o.o help me..e.e old crone."

"How might I be helping such a pretty mermaid?"

Gathering all her courage, Katina commanded royally, "I want to become a human, old crone and I know you hold the power to help me."

The old crone floating menacing to Katina laughed as she squeezed the worried mermaid's cheek and cackled, "Well! Are we not a brave sea-creature?" Moving her thin bony fingers through Katina's flowing hair, sneered, "What such beauty you have my young mermaid."

Shuddering at the old crone's touching her hair, Katina's repulsion was soon forgotten as she held several strands in her own hand. Agreeing with the old crone, Katina said, "My hair is truly beautiful."

Hiding a smirk behind her gnarled hand and as she floated from Katina, she cackled, "The mermaid is very vain and her hair is truly beautiful." Leering at Katina the old crone shrieked, "You come back soon … "

Katina's fear of the old crone gone and without regret she swam swiftly to the ugly sea-creature and then lovingly kissed the old crone's cheek. "I will come back!" Before the old crone could put a curse on her, Katina swam swiftly from the cave.

A hand on her cheek, the old crone stared after the mermaid.

"Hello! Katina!" Do you want to play some games?"

"Hello! Marla!" Swimming to Marla, Katina excitedly told her, "I have been to see the old crone!"

Marla exclaimed, "Katina! She could have put a curse on you!"

"I was not worried! I will be seeing her again!"

"You must not!"

"The old crone will not harm me, Marla." Floating happily around Marla, Marla flicked her tail teasingly at Katina.

For some time the mermaids played games and then bid each other goodbye.

Katina lay on her coloured coral bed and thinking about the old crone.

"I must seek the old crone again soon." Katina's longing to be back with Tom and Katie was becoming unbearable. Her eyes slowly closing … Katina slept.

Waking from her sleep, Katina went looking for her mother. She found her mother seated on her throne and swam swiftly to the queen. The smiling Queen on seeing her sad looking daughter her smile went from her lips. Floating from her throne, Queen Coral swam to the sad mermaid and asked, "Why is my young Siren again sad?'

Clinging to her mother, Katina cried, "Mother!"

Taking Katina's hand in her own, Queen Carol swam with her back to the royal thrones. Seating Katina on the King's throne, she said, "I know that you are missing the world above, Katina." At Katina's slow nod, the queen spoke sadly, "Your father, the King and I have watched your sadness and have known your heart's desire.

We have spoken much about your longing for the humans." Lightly squeezing Katina's limp hand, the queen spoke sadly, "Your heart belongs above the ocean … with your humans."

"Oh! Mother! I truly love you and father and do not want to leave you … but I must see Uncle Tom and Katie again, to live with them!"

Knowing how wise Katina had become, kissing her daughter on her cheek, Queen Carol commanded, "We must not speak of your sadness!"

Katina's hug of her mother was long. "I truly love you, Mother!"

Without speaking a word, Queen Coral slipped from Katina's hold then swam from the castle. Knowing her mermaid would not be with them forever, Queen Coral's crying was long.

Feeling happy about her mother's understanding of her heart's desire and not having seen her mother's tears and her sadness, Katina also swam swiftly from the castle in search of Marla.

It was an excited Marla who saw Katina first and called happily, "Hello! Katina!"

Floating to Marla, Katina teasing, asked, "Why are you so happy?"

"I hope you will also be happy for me …"

Interrupting the excited Marla and looking cheeky at her, Katina giggled as she spoke, "I will always be happy for you Marla."

Holding onto Katina's hand, the excited Marla said, "Ecnal has asked me to wed him!"

"You are truly worthy of such happiness and you be happy … always."

"I am also happy, Marla! My heart's desire will truly be!"

The happy mermaids frolicked until Katina floated beside Marla and said, "I am going to the old crone!" Amused at Marla's shocked look, Katina spoke hurriedly, "If I do as the old crone bids, she will grant me my heart's desire and …"

No! Katina! You must forget the old crone!"

"Marla! I truly want to live with the humans so that I can …"

Marla again interrupted Katina and taking hold of her hand, said, "If you truly want to be a human and it is your heart's desire, then I will be happy for you. We will always be friends."

The two mermaids sang and frolicked a while longer until Marla, kissing Katina on the cheek, said, "I must be going Katina."

Waving to Marla and as Marla began swimming away; Katina swam in the opposite direction. Reaching the cave of the old crone, Katina called, "Are you in there, old crone? I have come back just as you asked me!"

The old crone's voice sounded more evil as she called back, "You do not have to shout! I am here!"

Taken unaware by the sudden booming voice Katina tumbled backwards her hair floating across her face.

The old crone pushing Katina upright held several strands of black hair in her gnarled hand and cackled, "Will the beautiful mermaid do what I ask to have your heart's desire?"

Feeling the pull of her hair, Katina said, "I will do what you ask!"

Letting go of Katina's hair, the old crone hissed, "Then cut off your hair so that I can wear it!"

"No! No! Not my beautiful hair!"

Cackling, the old crone threatened, "It is to be your hair … or no human body for you! … Little mermaid!"

Sobbing, Katina cried, "You must not ask this of me! Ask for anything else and I will gladly give it to you!"

Tiring of her game with the mermaid and becoming angry, the old crone; without another word, swam swiftly back into her cave. Sneering, the old crone thought, "It be true what I hear about this ugly mermaid. Only a great love will make her lose such beauty." Twirling in a circle, the old crone again hissed, "So.oo.o! This mermaid will not; as it is spoken of, be the one to break the old water witch's curses." For a quick moment the old crone's evil heart felt a slight ache of sorrow but it went just as quickly.

In her cave, the old water witch watched Katina and the old crone in her cauldron. She hissed evilly at Sazoone, "The vain mermaid will not cut off her hair!" She began chanting, "The mermaid will not cut off her hair ... will not cut off her hair!" Her chanting became a loud cackling.

Having swum a long while, Katina swam back to the castle. Resting on her sparkling coral bed, she began softly wailing. She did not want her mother hearing her sadness and asking, "What troubles my young mermaid?" Knowing only the old crone could give her, her heart's desire, Katina wailed for a long time. She spoke angrily, "I will not cut off my lovely hair! I will be a mermaid forever!"

The old water witch having watched Katina's swift swimming from the old crone's cave, to her cauldron screeched at Katina's image, "Such is human vanity, my young Siren! Human love is strongest of all love!" With great glee the old water witch placed the images of Tom and Katie in front of Katina. Her surprise at seeing what she thought was real, stopping her wailing, Katina said, "I do love you so much, Tom and Aunty Katie."

Drooling into her cauldron, the old water witch not wanting to watch the smiling mermaid ordered the cauldron to look again on the old crone. Surprised to see the old crone smiling and sickened by such a sight, with evil glaring eyes the old water witch angrily stirred the cauldron to a thick brew.

Had the old water witch watched in her cauldron a while longer at the smiling Katina; her evil glee would have turned to a great rage.

The images of Tom and Katie gone, Katina floating from her coral bed began swimming from the castle.

Outside the old crone's cave Katina tried looking into the dark cave. Unable to see the old crone, she ordered, "Old crone! Show yourself!" Katina's demanding words echoed back at her.

The sneering old crone appearing suddenly before Katina, asked, "Well..l.l! And what is the lovely maiden wanting from this ugly one?"

Katina spoke more bravely, "I will cut off my hair and ...!"

Before Katina finished, speaking, the old crone darted back into her cave and was quickly back. Grabbing hold of Katina's arm the old crone, pushing the glittering coral scissors into the mermaids trembling hand, she screeched, "Go! Ugly mermaid!

Go and do what has to be done!"

"But how will you find me? … and …"

Shoving Katina from the cave, the old crone spoke evilly, "I am like the old water witch! I see all!"

The scissors held tight in her hand Katina swam swiftly in the direction of her favourite rock.

Chapter Eighten
(Marla, I must say goodbye to you now.")

THE CORAL SCISSORS beside her and not yet having cut off her hair, Katina sat on her rock for a long time. Knowing in her heart that to have her heart's desire, she had to do as the old crone ordered. Slowly the sobbing mermaid began cutting her hair. She was cutting the last strands when she saw Marla swim up to her.

When seeing Katina's hair spread across the rock, Marla's eyes opened wide in surprise and called, "Katina! What have you done to your beautiful hair?"

Katina answered, "It is what the old crone said I must do."

Not knowing how to comfort the sobbing mermaid, swimming closer to the rock, Marla gasped, "Oh! Katina!"

"As I can never return to the sea, Marla, I must say goodbye to you now." Reaching for Marla's up-stretched fingers, Katina cried, "Goodbye dear friend. You be happy … always.'

Marla flung herself onto the rock and holding Katina close, said, "Goodbye Katina! You be also happy." Slipping from the rock into the water, Marla gave a sad wave to Katina before diving deep.

Tears falling down her cheeks, Katina called, Goodbye Marla! Goodbye my friend and 'sister'!"

Katina waited for the old crone to come find her. A long while passed. There being no sight of the old crone, Katina's thoughts were becoming troubled. Impatient for the old crone to appear Katina absently touched the small shiny pearl she had earlier entwined in her short hair. What if the old crone had not been truthful? Giving a loud sigh, Katina thought about her King and Queen. She had found it hard saying goodbye to them but her mother and father knew it had to be…

"Give me your hair and hurry!" Katina was startled by the angry and loud voice of the old crone. Pushing the large glittering spiral shell up to Katina she ordered, "Put my hair into the shell!"

Hurriedly Katina placed every strand of her hair into the shell, she then pushed the shell to the old crone.

Pressing the shell possessive to her, the old crone screeched, "Before your heart's desire can be done… you must swim to the shore!"

Looking across the vast ocean, Katina asked, "How can I swim so far? I am a mermaid and it will take me a long while to reach the shore."

Not answering Katina the old crone; the shell still pressed against her darted a short way from the rock. Swimming wildly around in small circles the old crone then swam swiftly away.

The high foaming wave was coming towards Katina. Its hissing frightening her, Katina became more frightened as the giant wave covered the rock lifting her up and taking her with it. Squeezing her eyes tight as she waited for the wave to smash her onto the rocks, she accused, "Old crone, you have broken your promise to me!" Trapped in the wave, the frightened mermaid thought she was going to die. The wave was moving closer to the shore. It was slowing its speed and moving from around Katina. Katina drifted among the small waves that floated her gently between several large rocks.

Hidden from the shore by the rocks, the lonely mermaid waited for the shore to become free of the humans. Katina watched the human children play their games on the sand and thought of the old crone.

Many times Katina slept as she waited. Awaking to the silence of the shore and seeing no humans she slid further into the waves. Swimming to the shore she thrashed her fish body slowly onto the sand. Waiting for her heart's desire to happen, much time passed. The sky becoming dark, Katina was feeling alone and very afraid she began sobbing. Her sobs turned into her siren singing. Her song soft and musical as she sang…

"Oh! Ocean so wide! Ocean so deep! Put legs on me with dainty feet! Do not fail my plea, I pray! I must become a human this day!"

Singing into the night until she could sing no more, Katina called, "Why? Old crone, have you not given me my heart's desire?" Again her tiredness overcoming her, Katina's eyes slowly closing fell into a deep, frightened sleep.

Chapter Nineteen
(I heard our little mermaid singing)

Katie insisting she heard Katina singing the past two days, Tom was beginning to worry about Katie's health. "What is troubling you so, Katie? Perhaps you are coming down with a fever."

Shrugging aside her husband's concern for her, Katie roused, "Oh Tom! Do stop fretting about me. I know what I have been hearing … and it was our Katina singing."

Frowning, Tom said "Come, sit Katie, and finish your hot drink."

Smiling at Tom as she held her drink, Katie said, "I did hear Katina singing, Tom."

Giving a knowing grin at Katie, Tom quipped jovially, "I believe you did hear our young mermaid singing."

Thinking Tom was not believing her, Katie roused, "Do stop teasing me Tom!"

Quickly standing beside Katie's chair, Tom kissed her on her forehead. Taking hold of her arm, said, "Let us sit in the parlour beside the fire."

Tom and Katie sat contented on the long and soft cushioned sofa. Their lives had changed greatly, since Tom's finding their young mermaid Katina.

"I do miss Katina, Tom. If she were still with us, she would be a young lady now." Giving a sigh, Katie continued, "But our mermaid being of the sea, her age would be time-less.

Staring at the fire as he listened to Katie and knowing what Katie said was true, Tom answered, "If only our Katina could come home to us." His eyes wet from his unshed tears, Tom sighed louder as he said, "But alas! Our mermaid belongs to the sea."

Placing her hand on Tom's arm, Katie whispered, "Our Katina is coming home, Tom." Pressing her other hand to her breast, Katie smiled as she said, "My heart tells me this is so."

Wanting to believe Katie, Tom said, "We must keep praying for Katina to return to us." Katie's sudden movement had Tom asking, "What is the matter? Katie."

"I heard our mermaid singing!"

Closing his eyes, hoping to hear Katina singing, Tom thought, Until we see you again my little mermaid."

It was late when Katie asked, "Do you believe our Katina will get her heart's desire and become a true human with legs like ours?"

Grinning at Katie, Tom again quipped, "My dear Katie! I truly believe our young mermaid will become one of us and we three will live happily forever!"

"I also believe this Tom, but for now, I will make us a hot drink."

Leaning back on the settee, Tom hoped for his Katie's sake that they would see Katina again live happily together … forever.

In the kitchen as Katie waited for the kettle to boil she again heard Katina singing and thought, I know you are close little mermaid and I wish I could seek you out … but! I do not know where I would find you.

Putting the hot drinks and cakes on the doily- covered tray, Katie went into the lounge room.

Chapter Twenty
(The strange feeling in her feet as she stood caused Katina to giggle)

The waves thrashing along the shore woke the sleeping Katina. In the early morning light Katina looked quickly at her tail. Seeing her colourful fish tail was still there, she began to wail. Needing the old crone to hear her, wailing louder, Katina began to sing …"

Oh! Ocean so wide, ocean so deep, old crone! Where are my two legs with tiny feet? You failed me a moon away; please do not let it be too late, I pray.

The sudden paling of the sky looked strange to the lone mermaid and she thought, Am I going to die? Looking back up at the sky and then at the thrashing waves Katina tried pushing her fish body toward the water.

Trying several times with her tail slide herself into the waves, she could not feel her tail. Reaching down for her tail to help move it Katina felt a strange feeling come over her and again she thought, "Am I truly going to die?

Katina tried one more time to flick her tail. Wondering why she could not feel her tail, looked down. Seeing her tail gone and the two legs with dainty feet, with great excitement she exclaimed, "The old crone did not forget me! The strange feeling in her feet as she tried to stand caused Katina to giggle. Getting her balance she then skipped lightly in a small circle. Feeling strange looked down and saw the soft seaweed covering her small body gone and she was now wearing a dress like Katie.

"I thank you old crone for my heart's desire! Now the old water witch's spell will be broken. Let the castle again glitter and shine and Deara and Kram again become sea-creatures, to become husband and bride."

Before turning from the calming ocean, Katina threw a kiss and called, "Thank you old crone. My kiss is truly from my heart."

Stumbling excitedly across the uneven sand, Katina hurried her steps to Katie and Tom's house.

Such was Katina's happiness that she sang towards the sea,

To the brightening morning, Katina said, "Uncle Tom and Katie please remember me as I remember you."

Standing on the steps of the familiar green painted house of Katie and Tom, she looked nervously around her. Seeing the pretty colourful flowers Katina smiled wide. Holding tight to the door knocker Katina pushed it hard against the wooden door. Hearing hurrying footsteps from inside the house, her chest became tight.

It seemed forever to Katina before the door was opened. The door opening wide, it was a smiling Katie who held her hands out to the surprised Katina. Kissing Katina on her cheek, Katie said, "Welcome home my little mermaid. Uncle Tom and I have missed you so much." Holding each other close, Katie said, "Your hair may be short and you no longer have your tail but I remember you my little mermaid." Letting go of Katina, Katie called, "Tom! Come quickly! Our young mermaid has come home to stay!"

Not hearing Katie clearly Tom slowly standing from his chair, went to see what Katie was so excited about. Katie's strange behaviour of the past two days had him worried about her. He was beginning to think his wife was becoming more ill than he thought.

Seeing Tom's slow walking towards them, Katina happily called, "Hello Uncle Tom!"

The surprised Tom gasped as he stammered, "It c..can not be..e!"

"It is truly me Uncle Tom! I have come home!"

Tears trickling down Tom's age-worn face, he held Katina close.

Pushing Tom gently from her and holding her skirt slightly up to show him her dainty feet in their shiny blue shoes, Katina said, "I have two legs and feet like you and Katie!"

The three hugging each other, Katie again kissing Katina on the cheek, said, "Let us celebrate this most wonderful and magical moment.

And it truly was a most magical moment! The lights of the green painted house with the beautiful beds of flowers stayed on for many hours. There being so much to tell each other and their love keeping them awake, the three talked many hours until tiredness overcame them.

It was with great pride that Katie led Katina into the bed room with the wooden engraved cradle that was always kept neat for her return. "This is your bed room, Katie."

Katina fell in love with her bedroom but wondered at the baby cradle as she thought, Perhaps it was Katie's when she was a baby."

Katie stayed with Katina until Katina fell asleep, and then kissing her on her forehead, crept silently from the room.

Chapter Twenty One
(Breaking the old water witch's curses)

Katina's life as a human had begun. Her love for the sea was always in her heart. It puzzled her as to why she loved to spend many hours on the sandy shore. One evening while seated with Tom and Katie, she asked, "Why do I love the ocean?"

Katie looked at Tom and Tom in turn looked at Katie. It was Tom who asked, "Do you not remember from where you came, my mermaid?"

"I have always lived with you and Katie, Uncle Tom."

After Katina had said goodnight to Tom and Katie." and then left them alone, Katie whispered, "Tom! Do you believe our Katina has truly forgotten her life under the sea?"

"I believe she has, Katie." Tom was so happy to know that Katina was truly a human.

Katina's dream that night was of an old water witch and a dull castle and an old crone. "Why could you not have been a good water witch?" Woken by her own words and looking around her bedroom and seeing nothing there, smiling, she snuggled under her blankets, Katina slept. Katina dreamed of a world under the sea and of a magical happening, of beautiful mermaids, sea-horses and shiny castles.

Before the wave; carrying Katina, was out of sight the old crone, clutching the large shell holding Katina's hair, was swishing speedily to her cave. Many sea-creatures swimming out of her way to be caught among the foaming ripples watched fretful after her. Many sea creatures wondered about the glittering shell and what was inside it.

Inside her cave she placed the shell high on the jagged stone wall. Instead of the old crone's evil cackling, she began singing a soft song; a song of true love. Feeling the soft touch on her cheek, the old crone knew it was a kiss from Katina. As Katina's kiss touched the old crone's cheek the shell began glittering brighter. Waiting for something to happen and when nothing was happening the old crone's body shook with anger. Touching the golden strands at the back of her head the old crone went into a trance. In her deep voice she began humming and swaying in rhythm. Suddenly she swirled in circles. Swirling faster and faster the old crone's humming became more melodious. Just like a siren's calling to her love, the old crone's humming changed to words of love. Her words of love were for her sister Coral and their mother.

"I will love you forever Coral…my sister true!

We did not deserve our horrible fate!

If it is willed that I should die … I will truly save you.

It was I that the old water witch did hate!

Your kind heart has endeared you to all the sea.

Coral my dearest sister, I will set you free.

Love will defy all evil … far and wide!

Let you and I search my heart's calling before I die!

Mother! Father! My love for you will always stand!

Your fate will be blessed and grand!"

It was while the old crone sang that two majestic sea horses harnessed in their colourful sparkling straps floated graceful towards the old crone's cave. Suddenly! The sea bed began trembling causing rocks to fall forcefully from the dark cave. The old crone, unaware of the danger around her, continued singing her song of love.

The large piece of rock balanced awhile before falling heavily and hitting the old crone between her eyes. Her ugly body lay lifeless across the fallen rocks. The two sea horses floating to the cave opening eased their bodies through the opening. Gliding to the pitiful body of the old crone and gripping several strands of tangled hair in their mouths, the sea horses began pulling the old crone from the collapsing cave. Placing her body amongst the thick coloured anemones the sea horses floated slightly away. Watching the old crone for a short while the sea horses became startled by the large dark shadow suddenly floating above the old crone's body. The shadow coming closer the sea horses watched helpless as they saw John Dory's mouth opening wide. The big fish, eager to snatch the old crone in his mouth, floated closer to her body. It was the sudden swaying of the anemones around the old crone that distracted the John Dory causing him to float slightly upward.

The arms stretched upward from the body of the old crone were not old and scarred, but young and soft. Long flowing golden hair floated over the anemones. Sitting up, Dearra, her large green eyes sparkling, looked up in time to see the John Dory turn into her beloved Lyal.

Shocked by what almost happened, Lyal gasped, "My dearest Dearra! I almost harmed you!"

Laughing softly and with her hands held out to Lyal, Dearra said, "My dear Lyal, I was never in danger from you."

Holding Dearra close, Lyal whispered, "The old water witch's curses have been broken."

The sea horses floating beside the wide glittering mother-of-pearl shell carriage clipped it to their harnesses. Guiding the shell beside the happy couple the sea horses nodded their heads for Lyal and Dearra to settle themselves in the Royal shell carriage. Lyal and Dearra having done as they were bid the sea horses skimmed swiftly through the calm waters.

Seeing Queen Coral and King Trebor's castle the sea horses glided swifter. Stopping outside the glittering castle and after Lyal and Dearra swam from the carriage, the sea horses departed. Embracing her sister Coral and King Trebor, the four swam towards their mother, Queen Ahsram and their father, King Enahs.

Swimming swiftly to Dearra, Queen Ahsram, pulling her daughter close to her, spoke happily, "Welcome back my beautiful Dearra!" Turning to Lyal, Queen Ahsram said, "Welcome, Prince Lyal." Seeing Lyal frown, Ahsram told him, "When you were a mer-boy and your sister Lyreb was a mer-baby, the old water witch stole you both from your mother, Queen Shayla.

While the sea-creatures celebrated the undoing of the old water witch's curses, they were not aware of the thick dark wave holding the screeching water witch and the hissing Sazoone speeding toward the large dark rocks. There were two new black rocks and the evil water witch and her pet Sazoone disappeared forever.

There was much merriment when Dearra wed her Lyal. Seven mer-children held Dearra's wide veil. Four pretty mermaids swimming around Dearra, scattered small anemone to float around their new

King Enahs and Queen Ahsram ruled the darkest of the ocean which had now a bright and happy Realm. Queen Coral and King Trebor continued to rule in their Realm.

Much time passed ... none of the sea-creatures noticed anything strange about the two ugly black rocks imbedded in the darkened sea bed. Having ample bright and happy places to play their teasing games, the dark place was never visited.

King Lyal, with Queen Dearra, ruled his Realm justly.

It was with great joy that time passing, Queen Dearra gave birth to two mer-babies, a Prince and a Princess and they named the Prince Darraj and the princess, Katina.

Watching the sleeping mer-babies, Dearra whispered to her Princess, "My precious little one, we can never forget our beautiful black-hair mermaid, Katina. " Kissing the mer-babies, Dearra swam to her King Queen Carol gave birth to two mer-babies. Princess Ecila, being the image of her mother. Prince Ekalb was the image of King Trebor.

Soon after, Queen Coral gave birth to the pretty yellow-haired Norahs.

Norahs reminded Queen Coral of her lost black-haired mermaid. Norahs was as beautiful as the mer-baby Katina. Suddenly gazing at Katina's sparkling necklace hanging on the coral wall, Queen Coral noticed the largest of the jewels missing from the necklace. Smiling wide, she knew in her heart that in time she would meet Katina again. "Until that precious moment comes my young mermaid, I will rule my realm justly beside my King.

It was the laughter of the small voice that had Queen Coral smiling as she turned to greet her very own mer-baby.

The End